BROOMSTICK BREAKDOWN

MAGIC, FUR AND CLAWS
BOOK 1

EVE LANGLAIS

Copyright © 1st Edition 2010 Eve Langlais

Copyright © New Edition 2023 Eve Langlais

Cover art by © Atra Luna's Book Cover and Logo Art

Produced in Canada

Published by Eve Langlais

http://www.EveLanglais.com

ISBN: 978-1-988328-01-0

ISBN: 978 177 384 4350

ALL RIGHTS RESERVED

Broomstick Breakdown is a work of fiction and the characters, events and dialogue found within the story are of the author's imagination and are not to be construed as real. Any resemblance to actual events or persons, either living or deceased, is completely coincidental.

No part of this book may be reproduced or shared in any form or by any means, electronic or mechanical, including but not limited to digital copying, file sharing, audio recording, email and printing without permission in writing from the author.

1

THE MAGIC POWERING HER BROOM COUGHED AND sputtered. Sophia held on tight as she lost altitude and weaved drunkenly through the night sky.

"You've got to be freaking kidding me," she muttered aloud. Apparently spelling a broom while frazzled and rushed had unwanted side effects. Like becoming intimately acquainted with the ground.

Oops.

The pole clamped between her legs bucked, and she found herself fighting the fitful antics of her broom while trying to keep a grip on the wooden handle jerking between her hands. She cursed her bad luck in a language not fit for human ears, then spotted a bright service station easily visible in the dark. She prayed to the Dark Lord—"No road rash. No road rash."—and aimed herself toward the lights for an emergency landing. The last time she'd crashed her broom it had taken weeks to heal the raw patches. A natural flyer she was not, so much so that she'd even submitted a request for the rare and popular Ali Baba book of spells, thinking that carpet flying sounded a lot safer than the traditional witchy method of travel.

The ground rushed up to meet her, and with one last quick prayer, she used her feet to slow her momentum, stumbling several yards before she came to a halt on the pavement. *I didn't crash. Yay!* Glad to be in one piece, Sophia checked her cross-body bag—ensuring it had survived as well—before swinging off her broom and glaring at it. The problem quickly became evident. Most of the bristles had fallen out, along with the magic that imbued them with flight.

Shoot. Now how am I supposed to get to the Samhain event on time?

She still stared in consternation at her only means of transportation when a tall, dark-haired man walked out of the garage, stepping into the pool of light surrounding the gas pumps where she'd landed. He rubbed his hands on a rag, the corded muscles of his arms gleaming with sweat even though the air was somewhat cool.

Any other time, she would have taken the time to admire the way the fabric of his dark T-shirt stretched across an impossibly wide chest and clearly delineated a mountainous span of muscle. If her concern over being late had not overshadowed all thought, she would have also noticed the way his well-worn jeans clung snugly to his groin and thick and beefy thighs.

Oh, who was she kidding? Even amid a calamity, she couldn't help but notice how hot the mechanic was with his tanned skin, ruffled hair, and strutting walk. Usually, she would have enjoyed playing the damsel in distress, a routine that involved the shedding of clothes and inhibitions, but she had an appointment to keep, and while lateness ran in her blood, the senior witches of her coven frowned—with rather unpleasant results—on junior witches who couldn't show up on time.

Most people under the glare of fluorescent lights looked sickly. Not this babe, though. Vivid eyes peered at her from under dark brows, and the hunky stranger's full lips twitched as he gave her the once-over, a look that made her body respond with tightened nipples and moisture softening her cleft.

As she cleared her throat and blushed under his frank perusal, she drew her plump self up, all five-foot-two inches, and in a voice that emerged squeakier than intended said, "Um, hi there." Although she might be a witch of questionable morals, a witty conversationalist she was not.

Brilliant white teeth gleamed when he grinned at her, and a deep dimple formed in his left cheek that sent her awakening libido into full sexual crush mode and dampened her panties even further. *Damn, pity I can't bottle him because I'd make a fortune—after I'd enjoyed him first of course.* Her dirty thoughts made her blush even deeper, and she thanked the Dark Lord that the man couldn't read her mind, even if her body seemed unable to stop betraying her.

"Hello." His deep voice rumbled pleasantly, and Sophia fought an urge to shiver—and to throw herself at him, begging him to whisper naughty nothings with his sexy voice. She didn't understand her body's out-of-proportion reaction to this stud. Sure, he was hotter than molten lava, but since when did her hormones drool and scream at her to maul a stranger on sight? She usually required a drink and dinner first, at the very least.

She ignored how her body tingled and vibrated and got straight to the point. "Do you have a broom I could borrow by any chance?"

He cocked an eyebrow at her, and one corner of his mouth turned up in a lopsided grin. "A broom? Feeling a sudden urge to clean?"

Sophia blushed again and then remembered who she was. A witch, a junior one maybe, but a witch nevertheless, so he, a mere human, shouldn't mock her. She straightened her spine and tried to adopt a chilly tone and face, not an easy task with her rounded cheeks and full lips. "Yes, I need a broom, if you please."

With a look that said, "Whatever you say, lady," he went back into the open garage bay, and she found herself watching the hypnotic and enticing view of his ass in those tight jeans while he strode out of sight. *Sigh.* He really was a nice male specimen. Maybe she'd make a detour on the way back.

A few moments later, he brought out a monstrosity of a sweeper, its wooden handle and wide brush head covered in grease and dirt. He offered it to her, and Sophia wrinkled her nose, not making a move to touch the filthy thing. "You know the purpose of these things for most people is to clean, not create a bigger mess."

"This is a garage. We don't care if it's clean. We just use it to push crap out of the way." His tone and expression held a note of impatience. Funny, because she felt the same kind of annoyance.

"Well, I can't use that...that thing. Dammit, are there any stores around here that sell *clean* brooms?"

"Sure," he drawled with a lopsided grin. "Course they're all closed at this hour."

"Then perhaps you have something more suitable at your place?"

"You already wanting to come home with me?"

"No." While the prospect sounded tempting, she didn't have the time to fool around. The glare she hit him with melted the smile from his face and he dropped his mocking attitude.

"That's fine, I only have a vacuum there anyway." He returned his disgusting sweeper to the garage and called out to her, "Where's your car? Did it break down? I can tow it to the garage and we can take a look at it in the morning."

"I don't have a car. Why the hell do you think I needed a new broom?" she grumbled only to belatedly realize, because of the crease on his brow, that what she had said made no sense. To a human anyway.

She placed her broken broom in a nearby trash can, then crossed her arms, tapped her foot, and nibbled her lower lip, attempting to think of a solution that would allow her to still make the gathering on time. She couldn't afford to wait until morning when the stores opened. She'd started her trip late and would barely make it as it was. Broom flying, while allowing one to avoid obstacles and fly in a direct path, was very tiring and required frequent pit stops—at least she and her poor, aching ass did. Apparently, a full bottom made for great padding when on a wide seat but didn't count for much on a stick only a few fingers wide.

"Do you need a ride somewhere?"

His question and solution to her current dilemma made Sophia mentally slap herself in the forehead because, of course, she should have thought to ask the hunk if he had a vehicle. It made sense after all, given his occupation. However, she needed more than just a quick drive into town.

Lifting her chin, she smiled at him. "If you don't mind, then, yes, I do need a lift."

"Okay. Just give me a minute to close up, and then you can tell me where to drop you off."

How about the next state over? It was a good thing she'd learned the spells of forgetfulness and persuasion, for she'd need both before the next twenty-four hours were done. First to make him take her where she needed, then to ensure he forget he'd ever met her.

He shuttered his shop quickly and came strutting toward her dangling a set of keys. He gestured to her with a tilt of his head and walked off to the side of the garage. She followed, once again admiring the view of his ass. She stared so intently, her mind mentally x-raying the fabric of his jeans and wondering if he wore boxers or briefs, that she almost ran into him when he stopped abruptly. Catching herself, she looked up to see a monstrous truck in front of her. No exaggeration. The thing had been painted with a massive snarling beast, jaws open, teeth slavering, and emblazoned with the word *Monster*. The truck sat high—high enough that she wasn't sure how she'd get in, seeing as it lacked running boards—and it screamed, *I never grew up*. In other words, a total guy toy.

The mechanic-turned-chauffeur pulled open the passenger door and stood back to allow her to get in. She peered dubiously up at the high perch, wondering if there was a graceful way to climb in when the man stepped up behind her.

"Need a hand?"

"Is there a step-stool somewhere?"

"Nope." Then, he placed his two large hands on her hips and hoisted her into the cab of the truck as if she weighed less than a feather. Turns out, he wasn't just pretty muscle. Apparently, he had the strength to go with it.

"What are you doing?" Sophia squeaked.

He chuckled. "You're welcome."

Before she could say a word in reply, the door slammed shut. A moment later, he clambered into the driver's seat and placed the key in the ignition. He turned to her before starting the engine.

"So where to, Miss..." He trailed off enquiringly.

"Sophia." Actually, it was Sophia-Anne, but she'd shortened her name a long time ago.

"Nice to meet you, *Sophia*. I'm Aidan."

The way he said her name sent a delicious shiver through her. Damn, her hormones were in overdrive, and in the confines of the truck cab, his heated presence and subtle scent—soap and *man*—intoxicated her, making her mind shy from the question and instead go straight into a fantasy of him dragging her onto his lap and using his mouth for something other than talking.

"So, where do you want me to drop you?" he repeated.

She snapped out of her erotic thoughts, hornier than ever, and froze, unsure of an answer, knowing if she told him the truth—*I need you to drive with me for about eight hours or so, depending on traffic*—he'd just laugh and ditch her. She did, however, have a trick up her sleeve. A witchy one.

She'd made sure to brush up on the spell of persuasion before starting on her trip. The *Witchcraft for Dummies* book had highly recommended it—as well as the spell of forgetfulness—for those traveling long distances through a world not yet ready for the concept of witches and magic. At least they no longer had to worry about being burned at the stake, but then again, being dissected by scientists wasn't exactly a big step up.

Taking a deep breath, Sophia recited the words to

the spell of persuasion and imbued it with her innate power. With a flourish of her hands—and a mental apology for using him—she flung the invisible but magical result at him. Then she crossed her fingers, hoping she'd done it right.

2

S*HE REALLY IS A BLOODY WITCH.*

The little hottie—with curves made for worshipping with his hands and tongue—had arrived out of nowhere with a pitiful-looking broom. She'd even told him that she didn't have a car, hence her need for a new sweeper, but Aidan had still stuck around, interested to learn what she might do.

He'd never met a witch before, and though his kind was cautioned to stay away from them—a warning that even the youngest pups knew—Aidan was drawn toward Sophia. He couldn't say if it was basic curiosity or just the heavy lust that hit him the moment he laid eyes on her, but he'd decided to offer her aid, not at all suspicious that she might try anything on him.

Not until she spoke in a funny language and waved her hands in his direction, sending a tickling sensation brushing over his skin.

Had he not been so busy holding himself back

from ravishing her tempting body, he might have stopped enjoying the scent she gave off—part ozone swirled with flowers and vanilla—and actually processed the fact that it screamed *dark magic*. He hadn't, though. She'd smelled too delicious, temptingly so, and his thoughts had been all consumed with the idea of diving between her thighs and eating her up, especially since he kept catching tantalizing whiffs of her reciprocated desire that proved she wasn't immune to him.

Even more interesting, his inner furry friend liked her, actually more than liked. His inner beast yipped and growled in agitation, trying to tell Aidan something. Actually, the word that kept coming to mind was *mine*. Unusual behavior for his mostly behaved animal half, whose most common demands were *eat*, *hunt*, or *fuck*. Even odder, something about this scenario tickled his brain. He was sure he'd think of the reason why later.

He found it interesting that she didn't seem to have a clue he was a werewolf, and thus immune to her magic, a strange quirk of his kind, which left him with a choice. Did he laugh and tell her the spell she'd attempted had failed, or did he play along and see where she led him? If he was lucky, he would end up naked in bed with her and finding out why common knowledge said that shifters and witches weren't compatible—and hopefully proving them wrong.

But back to the matter at hand, his sexy little witch with her tattered-looking ride which had obviously experienced some type of breakdown, which he had to admit, made him want to laugh. He could almost imagine her zigzagging through the sky drunkenly, before crash-landing close to his garage. Her face when he'd offered his big shop sweeper? Priceless—and kissable.

Alas, she didn't want his mouth on hers but judging by her attempt at a spell, she did need something.

"Where do you need to go, sweetheart? Your wish is my command." He took a wild guess as to the purpose of her spell and almost laughed at the look of relief and delight that washed over her face.

"We need to make it to Covenhouse Inn before tomorrow night."

"Where is that?" The name didn't ring any bells.

"Next state over. About eight hours or so. We can take the highway most of the way."

He couldn't help but ask, "What's happening at this Covenhouse Inn?"

"Great big important meeting."

He could guess as to what, seeing as it was October thirtieth. "I see. Where's your luggage?"

She bit her lower lip. "Um, I pack light. Given it's a long drive, we really should get going."

"We've got plenty of time if it's not until tomorrow night."

"I don't want to be late. As it is, this pit stop's taken enough time that I'm sure to miss the event's breakfast." She pouted.

"I'll make sure you're fed." He had sausage ready to go.

"Can we go?" She looked at him with eager intensity and a hint of doubt. Was Sophia unsure if her spell was working? "This is important to me."

His impish side wanted to jokingly ask if she'd be meeting with the devil given tomorrow was Halloween, but he didn't want to scare her off by hinting that he knew what she was. Clearly, she didn't want him to know, and his wolf side growled in jealousy at the idea of her ditching him for another ride. Later, maybe he'd tease some more, for now, he did as the witch ordered and put the truck into drive. They did have a long way to go, and with the roads empty at night, they'd make great time.

Lucky for her—and him—he knew of the perfect pit stop on the way to her destination where they could stop for the night. Maybe even get a taste of the honey he kept smelling. His throbbing shaft couldn't wait.

Sophia kept sneaking glances over at Aidan. She admired his strong profile while combating the heat that suffused her at his nearness. She still couldn't believe her spell of persuasion had worked so well. She'd expected more questions from him for, after all, her spell wasn't one of pure obedience, but he'd meekly followed her command, a heady feeling indeed. It made her wonder what else he'd be amenable to. Her gaze strayed to his crotch and the bulge within.

A low growl startled her, a sexy sound that reverberated through her core. When she raised her eyes to him, his gaze remained fixated on the road, and she chewed her lower lip. Had she imagined it? At least it helped change the direction of her thoughts. Tempting as she found him, to take advantage of his body under these circumstances would be inappropriate, for it would be impossible to ensure his response was voluntary and not the spell forcing his willingness. Even the fact that it would be pleasurable didn't give her an excuse. The Dark Lord might reward bad behavior, but as a woman who'd been in untenable situations in the past, she had lines she wouldn't cross, eschewing proper consent being one of them.

"So, Sophia, where are you traveling from?" he asked, his deep voice full of gravel and bass.

She debated lying, but without her last name, and given the size of the city she lived in, he'd have a difficult time tracking her down. Besides, once she cast the spell of forgetfulness, he'd never even remember meeting her—what a pity. "Niagara Falls, right on the Canadian and U.S. border."

"Nice place."

"Yes, it is."

"What do you do for work?"

Again, what was the harm in telling him? "I work as a legal secretary. You?"

"I'm half-owner of the service station, with my brother."

"What do you do there? Push that broom you offered me?"

"Only when I lose a bet." He chuckled at that. "Otherwise, I'm wrenching on motors."

A thought occurred to her. One that she probably should have thought about before taking his autonomy away. "Do you need to call and tell him you won't be in tomorrow?"

"Nope. Happens to be my day off."

"Lucky me."

"Lucky you. Besides, I'd just filled up my gas tank and I love going for a nice drive. There's nothing like the open road and a rumbling engine." He cast a glance toward her. "Well, except maybe a drive with good company."

A knot of guilt formed in her stomach, and Sophia began to wonder if Aidan wouldn't have driven her even without the spell. He seemed like a genuinely nice guy, one who probably would have extended a helping hand or, in this case, a drive to a lady in need. Too late now to find that out now, though. She'd already cast the spell, and it would have him in her control for twenty-four hours. That is, if she'd done it right.

She'd never seen the persuasion spell in action and never cast it on anyone, so she had to be wary and watch for signs that it was wearing off sooner than it should. Or worse, that it was overtaking his mind to an extent that he'd never be free of her control. She didn't want that to happen. Not only did she not want a permanent, life-long minion, she also didn't want to be responsible for someone's loss of personal liberty for life. Doing it for a few hours was enough of a stretch of her morals.

They'd driven for only about two hours, chatting like old friends—one whose bones she wanted to jump—when he pulled off at an exit.

"Why are we stopping?" She could see his gas tank remained half-full.

"I'm starving." He turned his head to look at her for just a moment—long enough to give her a smile that made her stomach flutter. "Don't tell me you're not hungry, too. This is the place to find the best burger and greasiest home fries in the whole state."

"Oh." She realized her stomach could use refueling. She hadn't eaten since the morning.

He turned into a parking lot for a roadside diner and parked in the back with the rest of the trucks. Before she'd barely unbuckled her seat belt, he'd left the truck and made it to her side, opening the passenger's door for her. The man moved incredibly fast.

He offered a hand, and she took it, the heat of his skin lighting up her own. But when she looked down, there was still nowhere for her to step.

When she hesitated, he reached up and wound his other arm around her waist, then swung her down and out of the truck. She swayed for a moment when her feet touched the ground, and she automatically placed a hand on his chest to steady herself. Though he'd briefly touched her once already—when he'd helped her into the truck—that had been quick and from behind.

Now, their connection lasted longer, and they were face-to-face. More intimate. It had her sucking in a breath, both from the effortless way he kept handling her and how her body reacted to his nearness. She almost felt dizzy as her senses became overwhelmed, taking in his musky scent and the warmth that radiated him. Even through the fabric of his shirt, his skin exuded heat, scorchingly so, and her body responded by pouring a liquid languor throughout all her muscles.

Her gaze met his and locked. *Oh my,* the smoldering interest in that one look.

He brushed his fingers down her cheek, scorching a line down it, making her nerve endings tingle rapturously. She craned her neck automatically, inviting him to touch more, but he quickly shut it down by asking, "Ready to eat?"

"Hell yeah." Pity what she craved wouldn't be on the menu.

As if sensing her very naughty thought, he winked. "Then let me feed you."

Come to your senses! She was flirting with disaster. An off-limits man, thanks to her persuasion spell. She quickly snatched her hand away, as if scalded, and looked out toward the fleet of trucks and trailers in the parking lot.

"This place is sure packed for so late at night. Are you sure we can get in?"

"Yes, I'm sure."

When she failed to move, he reached out for her hand, lacing his fingers around hers, finally tugging her forward. Sophia, still dazed from being so near to him a moment ago, stumbled along in a fog, her crossbody bag bumping her hip as she tried to keep up. *What is wrong with me?* She'd never fallen so dumb from desire before. Lust she knew, but this...this *thing* she felt for Aidan? Whole different level.

Regardless of how hot he made her, though, she needed to stay cognizant of the fact that he remained under her spell, making him a forbidden treat, no matter how much her body craved him. *Keep your head on straight,* she chided herself.

Upon entering the bustling diner, Sophia became keenly aware of the fact that, besides the waitress, she was the only female amidst a roomful of men. More than one of the patrons craned for a peek, a few even dared to leer, and she heard more than a few grunts and murmurs of acknowledgment. On instinct, Sophia tucked herself closer to Aidan, who released her hand and slung a protective arm around her waist to mark his claim. It caused some of the men to turn their attention elsewhere. Not all, though. She shuddered when she made eye contact with the one who hovered over his plate, licking his cracked lips in her direction.

Aidan guided them to an open table against a wall and stood sentry while Sophia slid into the chair that faced the wall. He tapped the table. "Menu's printed on here."

She started to read it but stopped when he still hadn't taken a seat across from her. "Are you okay?"

"I don't like the way they're looking at you."

"Maybe they'd go back to their own business if you'd sit down and stop acting like you're looking for a fight," she suggested.

His eyes flicked to her, then back to the room, and finally, he sat. "Don't these dimwits have any sense of decency?"

Sophia blinked at him in shock and couldn't help the smile that bloomed. He sounded so...*possessive*. And she liked it, even though she knew she shouldn't. Still, she didn't want to stir up any trouble, so she tried to reassure him. "They're a bunch of truckers who spend most of their time alone, except when they stop for food, and they must not get a whole lot of women coming in here. They're just admiring a rare sight of something not dressed in a plaid shirt with a baseball cap." She tried shrugging it off, but the growl that emanated from his chest told her that he wasn't satisfied.

Luckily, the waitress approached the table, snapping gum while holding a pad and pencil. "Evening, Aidan. What can I get you and your lady?"

The woman's deep, gravelly voice suggested she smoked at lest two packs a day. She had a pencil stuck in her frizzy blond hairdo that had never graced the cover of any magazine, and she looked old enough to have birthed most of the men in the restaurant. But she offered Sophia a kind, reassuring smile and a wink that melted away some of the tension that had built inside her since entering the restaurant.

"We'll have two of your burger specials, Lena. The usual toppings for mine with a coffee. And the lady will take hers..." He eyed her questioningly.

"Fully loaded, with an iced tea, please." Screw calories. She'd given up counting a long time ago. Some women just weren't meant to be skinny and she did so enjoy her food.

"Good woman." Lena patted her on the shoulder before heading off to the kitchen, shouting their order out loud enough to be heard over the din.

Aidan was back to scanning the room with a glower, so Sophia quickly attempted to lure him into a conversation. "Come here often?"

Without looking at her, he replied, "I've got a hunting cabin in the woods not far from here. I've been hitting this place going in and out for the last seven years or so. The food is great."

This was an assessment she agreed with when it arrived and she took her first bite. Massive portions, dripping with greasy goodness. Sophia closed her eyes in bliss.

She heard a chuckle, and she opened her eyes to see Aidan grinning, his attention finally on her and not the other men in the place. "It's nice to see you know how to enjoy food."

As if the size of her ass hadn't ben enough of a clue.

Sophia shrugged. "I get grumpy when I'm hungry or forced to eat salads."

"I'll have to remember that," he said, implying they would partake of more meals together in the future.

Flustered and unsure of a reply, she stuffed a long French fry in her mouth, but the potato was too long and hung out of her mouth. Before she could suck it in, Aidan leaned across the table and bit it off, his lips brushing hers electrically. Sophia sucked in a surprised breath and began choking.

Several whacks on her back later and to the sound of Aidan's snickers, she managed through watering eyes to take a drink of water and calm her coughing fit. She glared at his smiling mien when he sat back across from her.

"Looks like I'm going to have to teach you to share without trying to kill yourself," he said with a low chuckle.

"How about you leave the food in my mouth alone," she replied tartly. Never mind her body had quite enjoyed the brief touch of his lips and was already thinking up scenarios where he ate whipped cream off of certain body parts. She stood abruptly.

"I need to use the ladies' room before we get back on the road."

Aidan stood as well. "I'll go pay the bill."

"Here, let me give you some money." Sophia stuck a hand in her bag to feel around for her wallet.

He tilted her chin up and gave her a smile. "My treat. I'll meet you at the front door when you're done."

Then he strutted off to stand in line at the register. Bemused, she walked across the room full of men, keeping her gaze down to avoid looking anyone in the eye. A tinkling sound caught her attention, and she looked sideways to see the main door open and a burly fellow in a checkered shirt come in. She ducked her head back down, wishing that having witchy powers would give her some courage. Her wish didn't come true, and she entered the ladies' room, which was, of course, empty. She quickly peed and was washing her hands when the door opened. Expecting to see the waitress—the only other woman in residence—her eyes widened in shock when she saw a blur of red behind her. She would have screamed, but a rough, smelly hand clapped itself over her mouth while a thick arm wrapped around her middle.

Caught like a rookie witch without the use of her powers, she could only be thankful she'd already emptied her bladder or else she would have pissed down her legs when a gravelly voice said, "Hello, pretty thing. You and me are gonna have some fun."

3

AIDAN PAID THE BILL FOR THEIR MEAL, INWARDLY grinning, quite pleased with himself. The look on Sophia's face when he'd bitten off her fry? Priceless. Of course, he hadn't meant for her to choke, but all in all, he enjoyed knowing he could affect her the same way she did him.

He walked to the main door to wait for her, but a nagging sense of something wrong made him do a *U*-turn and instead head toward the ladies' washroom. The closer he got, the more his wolf paced, his agitation clear.

Danger. Sophia needs us.

Not questioning an instinct that rarely proved wrong, Aidan barreled into the women's bathroom and stopped dead. The first thing he saw was Sophia's terrified eyes just visible above the meaty hand that muffled her. The second thing he processed was the sneer on her attacker's face, one he'd take pleasure in wiping off.

"Get out of here, boy. This don't concern you." The fucker dared to say.

"I disagree. Unhand my woman now." Aidan's tone emerged low and deadly. He flexed his hands and barely managed to restrain his inner snarling beast. Seeing Sophia in danger with so much fear in her eyes was doing crazy things to his usual iron control. He just hoped this could be settled without the need to go furry in public. The man smelled mundane, but that didn't always mean shit.

"Or what?" The burly beast laughed.

Aidan didn't reply. He showed him. In a lightning-quick motion, he closed the distance between him and the asshole who dared to touch Sophia, and punched him hard in the face.

Crack. The nose broke, and the bastard released a bellow of rage, releasing his hold on Sophia as he pressed his hands to his bloody face. "Mother fucker, you're going to pay."

"Really, big boy? I'd like to see you try." As he continued to taunt his foe, Aidan reached for Sophia, grabbing her by the arm and pulling her away from her attacker. "Go, wait for me in the hall while I *explain* to this piece of shit why he's never going to accost women again." *And I get a chance to assuage my bubbling rage over his nerve in touching what is mine.*

"But—" she protested.

While keeping an eye on the bloody brute, Aidan

gave Sophia a gentle shove toward the door. "Go. I'll just be a minute."

The sound of the door swinging shut brought a feral grin to his face, a lethal one that made the miscreant back up with his hands out. A plea for mercy that came too late.

Suddenly, someone wasn't so big and tough anymore.

"Sorry, man. It won't happen again. I swear." The man begged, but Aidan was deaf to his words. He couldn't clear his mind of Sophia's ashen face, trembling chin, and eyes that sparkled with terrified tears. He still felt how fast her heart had beat within her chest, and smelled the sour fear that had emanated from her pores.

"You're damned right it won't happen again." With that warning, Aidan hit him—over and over again.

SOPHIA STOOD SHAKING in the hall, listening to the meaty thuds coming from inside the women's washroom. Her terror only slowly faded. Since she'd discovered her magic, she'd grown cocky and sure she could handle any situation. This attack proved she still had much to learn, such as making sure no one caught her by surprise again. If Aidan hadn't charged in like a medieval hero—and overprotective alpha male—she dreaded to think what might have happened. She couldn't help a grim smile at the continued violence she could still hear. Some women might have argued against the savage retribution she could hear coming through the flimsy door, but Sophia wasn't one of them. The jerk deserved every smack Aidan gave him and then some. She liked to think that Aidan wasn't just saving her, but every woman the asshole might have thought about attacking in the future.

Now that she was safe, Sophia could admire the way Aidan's eyes had flashed in fury, and how he'd used the possessive words, *my woman*. If only that were possible. Had this been a first date, she'd not only be making plans for a second, but she'd also be taking him back to her place for a proper hero's treatment.

But as it stood, Sophia ruined any chance at any possible future with him when she cast her spell and caused him to become incapable of making his own decisions without her influence. She regretted it more than ever now. *Such a shame because the man just keeps getting hotter and hotter.*

The washroom door swung open, and the object of her thoughts stepped out. His anger and rage had made him seem to grow twice as big as before, and the hank of dark hair that hung over his eye gave him a dangerous air, but she didn't find him intimidating. Just hot.

He said not a word to her, just drew her into his arms for a hug.

"Thank you," she breathed, feeling relief in the safety of his strong arms.

"I'm sorry that happened. I'll do a better job protecting you from now on."

What? Something in his words worried her, and a sudden realization hit. Were his actions against his assailant not done by his own choice? Did he act as her guardian because of the persuasion spell?

In fact, why had he entered the bathroom at all? She hadn't been able to call out for help when that man's hand had been over her mouth, but the cry went through her mind and moments later Aidan arrived to rescue her. Then, Aidan had taught the man a lesson. She hadn't instructed him to, but she'd certainly wanted it.

There was only one explanation. Her spell had gone awry. If working correctly, Aidan should only be obeying verbal commands, but there he was, responding to her thoughts.

Had she turned him into an automaton?

The idea spiked fear inside her, but she tried to reason with her panic. *Even if it has gone awry, it's just for twenty-four hours. It will wear off. It has to.* She might be inexperienced enough to have miscast, but she wasn't powerful enough to have conjured a spell that would take control of him for longer than that. In fact, it was far more likely to wear off sooner. Something she now hoped for, even if it meant he'd dump her off on the side of the road. She'd prefer that—even being late to the coven event—if it meant he'd be free of her influence sooner.

With an arm tucked tightly around her while she

remained lost in her distressed thoughts, Aidan guided her out the back door and through the parking lot, back to his truck. He only released her after he'd opened her door, plucked her off the ground, and seated her into the cab.

She was about to thank him again, but he shocked her by leaning in and brushing his lips against hers.

She gasped. It was the briefest of kisses, but one that made all her nerve endings sizzle in pleasure. He backed away and shut the door before she could process what happened—or do the most foolish thing, and ask for another.

Oh, no. Oh, no oh no, oh no. She touched her tingling lips. It had been so quick, she almost wondered if it had really happened at all. But yes, it had, and it only further proved that her innermost thoughts and desires were influencing his actions.

She watched him deftly hop in his side, and he met her gaze before she asked, "Why did you kiss me?"

"Are you going to tell me you didn't want me to?"

It wasn't that she didn't want it. In fact, she did. And that was the problem. *She* wanted it, and he gave it to her. But what did *he* really want?

They couldn't know. Now while he was under her spell.

"You mustn't do it anymore." She said it firmly enough that he'd have to obey.

She sensed he wanted to ask her why, but she forestalled his questions by turning to the side and resting her head against the window, pretending to go to sleep.

Not likely given his proximity, but at least she didn't have to lie to him about why he should stop kissing her when all she wanted was for him to do that and more. Much, much—nakedly—more.

She had to give up on the sleeping act when they hit a bumpy patch of road and her head bounced off the glass.

"You okay?"

"Yeah." She rubbed her noggin and looked at the clock. Daylight would still be a few hours away.

"So, what are yo doing up at the Covenhouse Inn? Some big legal secretary convention?"

She laughed at that. A work retreat would be far less lively than a coven one. "No, it's more like a gathering of friends from all over."

"On Halloween?"

She stopped herself from correcting him that it was *Samhain*. If she did, then she'd have to explain the holiday, and potentially out herself as a witch. Instead, she replied, "Yes, a Halloween party of sorts."

To her relief, he didn't ask for more details. As they drove, he vocally engaged her in a variety of topics—none of them the kiss they'd shared—and she learned that Aidan was knowledgeable and witty, and able to make her laugh often. The miles flew by, as did the hours. When their conversation finally dwindled, she learned she'd nodded off. She startled awake to the first pink rays of dawn lighting the sky.

She snapped to an upright position when the truck slowed down and pulled into a roadside motel.

"What are you doing?" she asked as she straightened in her seat.

"I'm tired. I need to sleep for a few hours. Don't worry, we'll be on the road again by early afternoon and you'll be at the Covenhouse Inn in plenty of time."

She debated ordering him to go on, but the yawn he cracked behind his hand decided for her. He needed rest. Besides, he was right. They'd made great time, and a few hours of sleep in a bed sounded great.

"Stay in the truck while I get us booked in," was Aidan's lowly spoken command before he leaped out and took long-legged strides to the motel office. Since he seemed determined to use his credit card, she didn't protest his takeover of the situation. Instead, she took the moment alone to dig some cash out of her bag and hide it in his glove compartment—enough to cover their meals, the hotel, and his gas going both ways. She'd already taken advantage of him with her mind-control, she wouldn't also abuse that power by taking his money. But she'd at least let him *think* he was being chivalrous. Surely that counted as doing the right thing.

She had a hard time convincing herself that she was doing anything morally right in this dismal situation, so she turned her attention toward glaring at the decorative paper witches fluttering in the dirty window of the motel office. Such commercialism of a sacred holiday irritated. She imagined the pleasure she'd feel in setting them on fire, but she restrained herself. Besides, she had to admit that she didn't completely hate "Halloween." She at least loved the discount on candy she could buy the day after.

Her time with Aidan had distracted her from her jitters about attending her first Samhain event as a real witch. It had only been two years ago that her tiny quirks drew the attention of a woman who informed her she'd been gifted magic by the Dark Lord. Sophia's reaction at the time? Laughter, only Marjorie, an older woman who claimed to be a witch, had been quite serious. When Marjorie held up a finger with a flame dancing on the tip, she gained Sophia's rapt attention. From there, Sophia joined a small local coven and began her lessons.

For two whole years she'd trained, and now, as part of her advancement, she had the honor of attending her first Samhain bonfire—replete with naked dancing and an orgy with the devil.

She'd not yet decided if she'd participate in the final act of the event, not because she was a prude, but because she wasn't sure how she'd feel in the moment. Thinking about it now, though, it didn't appeal. The only sex she wanted was with Aidan. The yummy man who was becoming more interesting and attractive the longer she was with him.

When Aidan strutted out of the office swinging a big plastic keychain around his finger, he looked to be headed towards her door. Knowing she needed to keep her distance—she enjoyed feeling his hands on her too much—she opened the truck door, intending to hop out and meet him. A dubious glance below at the ground made her wish again for a step stool, but she was determined to do this.

She reached one hand to the door handle and kept the other on the "oh shit bar" and started to lower herself while holding on tight. The ground was even farther down than she thought. She stretched and stretched, sliding further and further off the seat, hoping to touch land with her toe at any moment.

Instead, she felt Aidan's arm slide around her.

As she'd expected, her body reacted, sparking alive in ways she'd never experienced before.

She released her grip on the truck and allowed him to place her down. For a moment, he held her against the rigidness of his body, setting off a trembling heat that made her sway toward him.

Maybe just one kiss... Her eyes closed and her lips puckered...

No!

Her body and mind were at odds with each other.

Luckily, Aidan stepped away, turning his back to her and gesturing toward the hotel. "This way."

Good. At least one of them was in the right headspace now. It occurred to her that if he was responding to her inner thoughts and feelings, then perhaps her rational mind thoughts were winning out over the carnal lust ones.

Even so, her unsated lust had her wanting to stamp her feet in irritation over the situation she'd created. *I could really use a rage room right about now. Anything to get some of this sexual frustration out!* She may have slammed the truck door a littler harder than necessary, but Aidan showed no reaction.

Ignorant of the storm that brewed behind him, he opened a motel room door and half turned to gesture her in.

Her brow creased. "We're sharing a room?"

"Last one left. We lucked out."

Sophia looked around at the nearly-vacant parking lot and whirled back to eye him accusingly. He just smiled at her innocently.

"Are you telling me the truth?"

She could have sworn mirth twinkled in his eyes as he replied. "Of course I am, sweetheart. Do you think I'd lie to you?"

No, she didn't think he would—or could. The sway of her spell prevented him from being able to lie, but when she swept into the room, she stopped dead.

"There's only one bed," she exclaimed. A queen-sized bed, but still one bed only to share with six-foot-something of male yumminess. Her pussy creamed in excitement. *Down, kitty. Remember the spell. I mustn't take advantage of him. It wouldn't be right.*

Apparently, the prospect of sharing the bed with her didn't seem to interest him one bit. Never mind the kiss back at the restaurant, for, without even a look at her, Aidan stripped out of his shirt and kicked off his boots before stretching his body out on the bed, his eyes immediately closing.

Seeing the bare muscles of his chest exposed so temptingly, she fought an urge to take a flying leap on him just to lavish his body in adoration. No, she couldn't allow herself to be distracted from her mental vow not to give in to her desires.

"Do you need the bathroom before I go for a shower?" Cold water was the only way she could think to cool her licentious thoughts, plus it would give him time to fall asleep.

"I'm fine."

"Okay." She walked by him and closeted herself in the small, but clean, bathroom.

It didn't matter if she used cold or hot water, the shower did nothing for her raging libido, not when her thoughts kept straying to the fact that a hunk of male perfection lay just a few feet away, half-naked. And she couldn't stay in there forever. How could she crawl into bed with him and somehow not ravish him?

Impossible given the state of arousal she currently found herself in.

She wished she knew a spell that could quell her lust.

Well... she might not know a spell, but she did know one way to handle a situation like this.

Sophia leaned against the cool tile wall and took matters into her own hands, literally. She ran her hands over her rounded body, the water making her skin slick. She cupped her heavy breasts, squeezing them, and while her touch felt nice, she couldn't help but think it would feel a hundred times better if Aidan's callused hands were the ones fondling her. Her nipples hardened instantly at that thought, their pointed peaks perfect for a mouth to suck on.

Sophia sighed and closed her eyes, allowing the fantasy of the stranger in the next room to take hold. If he weren't under her magical sway, what fun could they get into? She imagined exiting the bathroom, naked and dripping from her shower. She'd clear her throat, causing his eyes to open and his gaze to land on her. That bit of desire she was certain she'd spotted back at the diner would return, amplified. She wanted to see him absolutely *craving* her. She'd tease him, straddle his bare chest, dangle her tits in his face, and then smother him with them. She'd guide one of his large masculine hands down her body to her cleft as his mouth pleasured her areolas, and he would use those strong fingers to stroke her clit.

Sophia's hand slid between her thighs to work her sensitive nub, and her breathing came faster. *Oh yes.*

Aidan seemed like he'd be the impatient type. The kind of man who would flip her onto her back, his mouth capturing hers in a kiss as his cock found her sex and plunged in, stroking her deep and hard.

Sophia mewled as her fingers penetrated her channel and worked in and out. Her whole body quivered with excitement and arousal, her pussy slick with her juices. She tilted her hips, trying to give herself deeper access with her fingers, but her orgasm hung just out of reach.

She continued on in her fantasy of Aidan plowing her, his heavy body above hers pumping away while his hands roamed every inch of her. He'd hold her legs up so he could penetrate deeper, his hard cock filling her up.

That's it, do me. Her visual fantasy made her pant while her body thrummed in pleasure. Faster and faster, she pumped her fingers in and out of her channel. Still, her orgasm remained elusively out of reach.

She mewled with frustration. *Why can't I come?*

4

THE MOTEL HAD PLENTY OF EMPTY ROOMS, BUT AIDAN asked for just one. There wasn't a chance he'd get a wink of sleep if separated from Sophia.

Why not?

He asked himself this question while the front desk clerk processed his credit card and made a photocopy of his ID. The most obvious reason was that he wanted to seduce the sexy witch—he definitely wanted a chance for a taste of her and he was pretty certain she wanted him just as much—and that would be a lot harder to accomplish if she were in another room. This line of thinking made the most sense to him.

There was also the protective instinct that had yet to abate after the run-in with the diner goon. If Sophia were separated from him, he'd be on-edge, worrying about her safety all night. This excuse he also understood.

What caused him the most alarm was the fear that

if they went into separate rooms, she'd be gone in the morning. Why did that idea bring distress him so much? Sophia was merely a stranger. One who'd attempted to put him under her spell and compel him to do her bidding. Why should he care if she took off?

It's not like she'd be able to escape me. Now that I have her scent, I can track her to the ends of the Earth.

That right there was the problem. He shouldn't have such intense and possessive thoughts about a woman he hardly knew. He'd never been the stalker boyfriend type. Never obsessive about the women he slept with—or wanted to sleep with. So why now? It was almost enough to make him wonder if something in her spell had actually worked, but he knew better. Witch magic had no effect on shifters, yet his mind had been running circles around this idea for the whole drive.

There was only one conclusion. One he couldn't deny any longer.

Sophia is our mate. The woman we're meant to spend the rest of our life with. His wolf had been trying to tell him this the whole drive, but Aidan had stubbornly ignored it.

He couldn't believe it. Apparently, the lore his father had handed down about mates had been true. When you met *the one,* your shifter side instantly knew —if you were one of the lucky ones to ever cross paths with your mate. True mates weren't common. With thousands of wolf shifters scattered around the world, what were the chances a wolf's mate lived within the pack or even nearby? Some left the pack, questing for years in the hopes of finding the one who would complete them, a few even succeeded. Most—like Aidan's father—just ended up settling for an attractive bitch and popping out a few pups.

Had Aidan's wolf known upon first meeting her? The man side certainly hadn't. When he first laid eyes on her he'd found himself instantly attracted and in lust, but that wasn't an unusual reaction. He had a healthy sex drive and she was definitely hot, but the more time he spent in her proximity, the more overwhelming became the urge to touch her, taste her, *mark her... claim her.*

His wolf, not usually interested in the other sex beyond fucking, kept wagging his shaggy tail inside of Aidan's mind. Agitated and excited, he'd attempted to make the thoughts in his bestial mind known to Aidan. *Claim her, mark her, make her ours.*

The revelation had stunned, and he was thankful she'd been snoozing when it hit and the truck swerved on the road.

However, the knowledge that Sophia was meant to be his came with a slew of problems—the first and foremost being the fact that she wasn't a wolf, and members of his pack weren't permitted to marry outside of their kind. Punishment up to and including banishment was a distinct possibility if Aidan pursued her—even if fate had determined her to be his true mate. And that didn't even factor in that even if the pack somehow overlooked that they came from different genomes, Sophia—lacking the same mate sense—might not be interested.

Aidan might be driven by a mystical reaction that urged him to make a life pact and commit himself to forever with Sophia, but that didn't mean she felt the same. Heck, he had no idea how the true mate bond affected a non-wolf, if at all.

Which brought him back around to the fact that his sexy mate still didn't have a clue as to Aidan's origins and true nature. While she might not be a regular human, the witch might balk at having a husband who turned furry on full moons and whenever else he had the impulse to chase things through the woods. Would it assuage her doubts to know they now had products for dealing with fleas, and Aidan wasn't the kind of shifter to come inside with wet fur?

Itemizing the reasons a mating wouldn't work proved to be futile when his shifter side—*oh yes blame it on the wolf*—forced him to think of reasons why it *might*. No denying the clear evidence she desired him, the most powerful being the heady scent of her arousal that lingered throughout the drive and amplified each time he helped her in and out of the truck.

Not to mention, how it had become overpowering after he'd kissed her. The smallest graze of lips-on-lips, yet it had an extraordinary effect on both of them.

He left the little motel office, swinging the old-fashioned key around his finger while his mind nearly drowned in all the strange new thoughts. He spotted Sophia trying to slide out of his monster truck and knew immediately it would end in a broken ankle, so he sprinted the few yards to help her down.

Only this time, the moment he touched her everything inside him screamed for him to take her and make her his. To claim her so the rest of the world would know, too. To not even wait until they were in the hotel room—just strip her there and fuck her against the truck, leaving the mating bite on her shoulder while they both climaxed and she screamed his name.

Obviously, that wouldn't go over well, not with Sophia, and not with the motel clerk or any of the guests who might look out the window and see their indecent exposure.

He quickly turned away from her, realizing he needed to play it cool if he could hardly touch her without losing control. He'd have to wait for her to come to him, for her to make the choice to be with him, because once they finally coupled, there would be no going back. He'd bite her and mark her as his forever.

He led her to their motel room with a slight pang of guilt over lying to her about it being the last room available. He feigned indifference when he noticed her nervousness at the realization they'd not only be sharing a room but a bed too, and he pretended not to notice her staring as he'd stripped off his shirt and kicked off his boots. He had to stretch out on the bed and close his eyes immediately, otherwise, his nonchalant act would have quickly faltered and his thin grasp on control would have failed. The quick brush of his lips on her back in the truck in the diner parking lot would have been nothing compared to the way he wanted to devour her now. Her sweet arousal called to him. He knew she wanted him, but something was holding her back from acting on it.

When she moved on to the bathroom he was left alone with his thoughts again. It astounded him how strong his feelings were toward her now that he'd embraced the truth. Sexual attraction he could deal with. Hell, he could bang it away, no problem. But Sophia offered more than that. Apart from wanting to screw her until they both howled, he also found her intriguing, cute, intelligent, and just about perfect so far.

How did she view him, though? Despite her sexual interest in him as a man, he couldn't miss her trepidation. And that was without her even knowing his other nature, the fact that he was a man with a wolf inside. A human who could transform into a furry beast.

How should he approach the matter? *Hi, just so you know, I'm a werewolf and you're my true mate. Let's fuck so I can bite you and make you mine forever.*

Hmm. It occurred to him that Sophia must be a new witch, one inexperienced enough to have the kind of broomstick malfunction that landed her at his garage, and also naive enough to not know when she was trying to spell a shifter. What if she didn't even know about the existence of his kind?

A strange thought. Aidan had grown up with wolf

parents, brother, and pack, but perhaps Sophia hadn't been raised in a witch family. It would explain why an adult witch of her age made such missteps, and also why she hadn't slung spells at the diner goon to protect herself.

In that case, the direct approach probably wouldn't work. He didn't want to scare her off. However, how did one explain to a woman he'd just met that they were destined to live happily ever after? Oh, and how did she feel about having puppies? Or not. Perhaps they'd not be able to have offspring at all. Fertility issues were one of the reasons interspecies matings were frowned upon. No matter. While Aidan had always figured he'd have children, he hadn't been set on it. The only thing that mattered now was making sure Sophia stayed in his life.

His ears prickled at the sound of the water turning on in the bathroom. Instantly he pictured her curvy body under the spray, naked. His erection sprang back to life, throbbingly so. Damn, he'd have to do something about this mate thing soon. His control was wearing thin already, and he'd met her only hours ago.

The easy solution? Fuck her.

The problem? Would it be possible to keep enough control during the act to not mark her? Unlike others of his brethren, he wouldn't force his bite on her. He needed her to have the facts so she could decide on her own.

The very idea tested his patience, but he had to

figure that fate wouldn't have chosen Sophia if she wasn't destined to feel the same way about him?

Would it hurt if he played a little dirty in his quest to have her see him as more than just a ride to a witches' convention? He unbuttoned the top of his jeans to give his cock a bit of room to breathe. Once again, though, his mischievous side, which was determined to move things along, had him shucking his pants completely so he wore only his black briefs. Unlike some others, he couldn't go commando. His goods took up enough space down there to make him nervous about zippers.

Lying back on the bed, he allowed himself to run his hand over his cock, as though that might help anything. All it did was increase his desire, which heightened even more when his sensitive shifter hearing picked up her soft moans. He sat bolt upright in bed.

No. She can't be.

Another mewl. Soft enough the average human wouldn't have heard, but his wolf hearing sure did.

She is! His mate was pleasuring herself in the shower. Fondling her body, stimulating her clit, penetrating her cunny—without him.

He began to work his hand up and down his erection, wanting to release with her, until he realized that her cries weren't mounting toward a climax. He heard the frustration in her small sounds. Apparently, his little witch needed more than the stimulation of her fingers.

He smiled to himself and wrapped his fingers around the base of his cock, squeezing and using the pressure to steady himself. If she wasn't getting much-needed relief, then neither was he.

The idea of barreling through the flimsy bathroom door crossed his mind, but he had to stick to his guns and wait for her to come to him. He still for the life of him couldn't figure out what was stopping her from asking him to pleasure her. He'd been kind. Played along with her witch spell game. Driven her with nary a complaint. Defended her against the diner goon. What was holding her back from being with him?

Maybe he could ask. Maybe she'd be willing to talk about it and work it through. Then, he could relieve their sexual tension. He could control himself long enough for that. And if the urge to bite grew too strong...well, he'd worry about that dangerous cliff when he arrived at the edge of it.

SOPHIA SAGGED in the shower and admitted defeat. Much as she wanted to and tried, she couldn't come. But at least she'd been in the shower long enough for Aidan to have fallen asleep.

She turned off the shower, stepped out, and toweled herself dry. She'd brought her bag into the bathroom with her. She opened it and scrounged around inside.

The cross-body bag, though not extraordinarily

large on the outside, was much bigger than it seemed on the inside. She reached her arm inside up to her shoulder and dug around to find her sleep T-shirt and shorts. Earlier she'd told Aidan she packed light, but he had no idea she owned a magic bag with room enough to store her entire closet of clothes if she wanted. One day she planned to master the spell so she could turn her tiny apartment into a massive penthouse.

She dressed in her night clothes and shoved her dirty clothes in the hamper she kept in her bag. In there she also had a medicine chest, a supply of snacks, and some random stuff she might need—like a razor for her legs since she'd yet to grasp the spell for shaving.

She stalled for time by scrubbing her teeth and running a brush through her damp hair. She even rubbed moisturizer over every inch of her skin. *This is stupid. I can't stay in the bathroom forever. He'll be asleep for sure by now, and even if he's not, it's not like he'll know I'm horny. The guy's been a gentleman this far. All I have to do is keep my rational thoughts at the forefront and project to him the order: no sex!*

Taking a deep breath, she opened the door and exited the bathroom. The sinking feeling in her stomach when she saw him sleeping on top of the bed in his underwear definitely wasn't disappointment.

Who could be disappointed when the most perfectly shaped man ever to grace the planet lay on the covers wearing only black briefs that did little to hide an impressive bulge, one that seemed to grow and twitch as she watched it with wide eyes?

Sophia swallowed the extra moisture in her mouth but could do little about what pooled in her sex.

He moved on the bed, rolling on his side to face her. He opened eyes that she could have sworn glowed and said in a low, husky tone "Come to bed, Sophia."

Her cleft quivered in response.

She wanted to shake her head, say no, run away from the blatant sex appeal he oozed. But as if he had *her* under a spell of persuasion, she found herself taking one step after another toward the bed until her thighs pressed upon the mattress.

She still couldn't speak. She could only watch him as he rolled onto his back, his eyes never leaving hers.

"Get into bed," he said in a voice that was almost a growl—and was most certainly a command.

When she didn't comply, he moved quicker than she could follow, grabbing her and pulling her onto the bed. In the next breath, she found herself flat on her back with him atop her, his heavy weight pressing down on her deliciously.

"What are you doing?" The dumb question came out of her mouth as she writhed underneath him—not trying to get away from him, but wanting to rub every inch of her body against his firm form.

"I promised myself I would give you time." He traced her full bottom lip with one finger as he looked down at her. "But I find myself unable to resist you."

He bent his head, enveloping her lips with his, his body pinning hers, his hands caressing every curve.

And Sophia forgot all her good intentions.

Screw waiting until she knew all the facts. Every second she delayed leaving the bathroom increased his desire. When she'd finally stepped back into the room with him, the scent of her arousal was too much. He couldn't feign sleep. He couldn't maintain distance.

He opened his eyes. There she was. His mate. So soft and alluring, with her eyes clouded in longing and confusion. He couldn't help himself. And as if proving that they were connected, that she might not be a wolf shifter but she still knew they were meant to be together, she'd obeyed his order to approach, even if trepidation made her pause before joining him in bed.

He would make love to the witch who would be his mate. He'd enjoy it, and so would she. There wasn't anything objectionable in that, so long as he held back from marking her as his mate. He could control himself that much…he hoped.

The first taste of her lips set him afire. Hunger of the carnal kind raced through his body and imbued his kiss with some of his urgency, an urgency she returned as her lips clung to his.

"We really shouldn't," she murmured as her hands clung to his shoulders like they were a raft and she was at risk of drowning.

He looked into her eyes and saw the doubt, but her undulating hips beneath him told him that whatever was forcing her to hesitate wasn't strong enough to request he stop. She wanted him. Her body needed him as much as his needed her.

"Shh." He kissed her again and settled himself firmly between her legs, grinding against her mound.

She tilted her hips and rocked, as clear an invitation as her moan was, and his cock managed to free itself through the folds of his briefs, searching for her slickness. Her minuscule sleep shorts had already ridden up, and she splayed her legs wide enough for him to rub his cock between the fabric and her skin, and push them aside so he could access her fully.

When his silky head slid against her velvety folds, she gasped, pulling back from their kiss and arching beneath him. Her nails slid off his shoulders to dig into his back, and her body repositioned so their sexes aligned.

Seeing her in such rapture was enough that Aidan almost bit her then and there, almost penetrated her

Shit. He was in trouble already, his wolf awake and pacing, waiting to take over and mark their woman. He had to readjust. Put himself in a less dangerous situation. Perhaps if he made the pleasure all about her, he could hold off biting her.

To her disappointed cry, he disengaged, pulling back from her sex, propping himself on his knees and tucking his cock back in his briefs. He focused on her, sliding his lips down the smooth skin of her neck. He could feel her pulse under her skin, fluttering. With no control over it, his canines descended, the urge to bite almost overcoming his will.

Oh fuck. He moved down from the site of his future claiming mark, away from the temptation that beckoned. The fabric of her T-shirt was such an unpleasant sensation after the feel of her skin that he had to get rid of it. With a growl, he tore it off her, revealing her ample and beautiful breasts to him.

She made a slight sound of protest, but that quickly turned to pleased moans when he took a breast in each hand and began to caress, soft strokes at first, but then rougher squeezes, teasing around her nipples.

"Yes," she sighed, reaching above her to grasp the pillows, baring herself to him, giving him free rein. She didn't add it, but he could hear the *please* that she dared not speak.

He turned back to look at her globes, heavy and round. Her big nipples puckered at his view and begged for his touch. He dipped his head, flicking his tongue on one, then the other, then rubbing his rough calloused thumbs over both until she moaned and panted.

He tucked one taut peak in his mouth and sucked hard. Her frantic hands clutched at his head, weaving through his hair and then tugging. The pain only heightened his own desire.

He bit down lightly, and she let out a small scream. Once again, his canines tried to descend and puncture the sweet flesh that tempted him.

No.

He had to be stronger. Build her trust. Get her to accept him. Fuck her brains out 'til she'd do anything he wanted.

With a groan, he released her nipple from his mouth and moved his lips down her body again, over her soft belly while he squeezed the supple flesh of her hips.

His nose was so close to the source of her lusty scent. His mouth salivated and continued on, moving like a heat-seeking missile to find her core. Her shorts covered her mound, and his hands tore them apart just as easily as he'd done her T-shirt.

She responded with a cry, and by pinching her thighs pinched together, a sign he took for shyness. He could fix that. He began coaxing her slowly by kissing each of her legs and nuzzling her pubis. The prize was so close he could taste it, but he wanted to *actually* taste it.

"Open for me, sweetheart," he encouraged, and to his delight, she did, dropping open her legs and exposing herself with a breathy sigh.

Her glistening sex beckoned to him, and he took a moment to enjoy the view before touching her gently with a single finger, running it along her folds, exploring the most sacred of all places.

His tongue yearned for that first taste, and he treated himself to a lick of his finger.

The flavor exploded on his tongue, and his wolf nearly screamed inside him, *mine, mine. All mine.*

He pushed her thighs open wider, and crouched, moving his face into position, ready to sate his appetite and bring his mate to climax.

Bad idea.

With his face between her thighs, her scent overwhelmed him, and his canines descended again, their sharp points almost nipping his lip. He took several shuddering breaths as he tried to regain control, but all that did was draw her scent deeper into him.

She noticed his lack of action and rolled her hips in invitation. With a sound that was part-mewl, part-moan, she called to him, "Please."

What could he say? He didn't have the willpower to refuse his mate. Screw his good intentions. He'd give her what she wanted and deal with the repercussions later. "Your wish is my command, sweetheart."

5

Sophia froze at his words, her ardor dampened as if a cold bucket of water had doused it. *That damned persuasion spell.* This wasn't right. She couldn't do this to him. This was a man under her thrall. A man who she knew hardly anything about. What if he had a wife or a girlfriend back home? How could she know this was what he wanted and not the spell getting mixed-up signals from her desire, forcing him to do something he'd regret?

"I can't do this."

Though his hands had gripped her thighs tightly, he released her in shock, looking up at her with questioning eyes.

"I'm sorry." She scooted off the bed and streaked to the bathroom, grabbing her bag on the way. Only when she slammed the door shut did the shaking start.

A second later, a knock sounded. "Sophia? Are you

okay? I'm sorry if I was moving too fast. Don't hide, sweetheart."

Sophia didn't answer; she just shook harder. *What was I thinking?* Well, she knew what she'd been thinking: *Ride him like a cowgirl until the cows come home.*

Bad witch.

It didn't matter if he seemed a willing participant. Her spell had skewed his normal responses, made him somehow think he also had to fulfill not only her verbal commands but also her unspoken bodily ones. *I almost took advantage of him.* While she could excuse using him as a chauffeur, using his body—that crossed a moral line.

"Open the door," he pleaded.

"No."

"I'll kick it down if you don't come out here and explain what's wrong."

Sophia began to laugh hysterically, even as tears streamed down her face. *How do I explain? By the way, I'm a witch and I've cast a spell on you, so while you think you're horny right now, it's probably actually my hormones you're feeling. Sorry for messing with your brain.*

She screamed when the door splintered open. Aidan looked huge and angry; his form filled the doorway. At the sight of her huddled on the floor, his face softened.

"Aw, sweetheart, don't cry. I'm sorry if things moved so fast. Come back to bed. I promise we don't have to do anything, okay?"

"It's not your fault," she managed to sputter. She

wanted to tell him that she was the one who couldn't be trusted—*I'm no better than a bloody succubus*—but she said nothing and didn't protest when he scooped her into his strong, protective arms, and carried her back to the bed. He placed her down gently, tucking her into the sheet and blanket, then eased himself behind her, on top of the covers to keep a barrier between them. A heavy, warm arm wrapped around her waist and spooned her back into the scorching warmth of his body, and she let out a whimper.

Oh, why does he have to feel so good?

He misinterpreted the sound and shushed her. "It's okay, sweetheart. Go to sleep. I promise to behave."

Sophia lay stiffly in his embrace and struggled to understand this enigmatic man. To her puzzlement, she still felt the evidence of his arousal against her bottom where she was snuggled into him, and this even without her pawing at him. *Is it possible he actually wanted me and not because of the spell?* No. That was just her wishful thinking. Not that it mattered. She refused to take the chance.

Besides, the spell was just the tip of the iceberg of her complicated feelings toward Aidan. Her reactions to him had been overly intense from the first moment she'd met him. While she'd experienced attraction and lust in the past, desire like she experienced with Aidian had never completely overwhelmed her before. She was acting as if bespelled—*or maybe I'm falling in love*, she thought—and it scared her.

People don't fall in love in one day, she reasoned. It

couldn't be love. But what other explanation was there for the extremely heightened draw she had toward him?

It wouldn't matter if it *were* love. In fact, it wouldn't matter if she hadn't spelled him. Sophia and Aidan would never have had a future, because witches aren't supposed to fall for humans.

No matter how sexy.

She knew the rules, and it took chanting it to herself over and over for her to finally slip into a restless sleep.

SOPHIA WOKE a few hours later when Aidan left her side, even though he'd moved slowly and cautiously. She let him go, pretending to still be asleep until he shut himself in the bathroom.

If she were smart, she'd leave right then. But how would she get to the gathering? Steal his truck? It would be easy—he'd left his keys right there on the table, along with his wallet and cell phone.

No, she could never do that to him after all she'd already done. Plus, she still needed to spell him to make him forget.

The sound of the shower galvanized her, and she extricated herself from the bed, found her bag, and pulled clean clothes from it. She dressed quickly, then returned to the bed, sitting cross-legged while trying to concoct a good explanation for her hysterics of a few hours ago. She took a few deep breaths to help compose herself, and by the time the shower stopped, she almost felt ready to face the music.

Her heart rate picked up while she waited for him to emerge, and all her poise vanished the moment she saw him fully dressed with his dark hair damp and slicked back.

Why does he have to be so bloody gorgeous?

She readied herself for the apology and explanation, but it all ended up unnecessary, for when he spoke it was only to say, "Ready to go? We'll grab some food on the way."

He barely glanced in her direction as he scooped up his property from the table, shoving his wallet in his back pocket, phone in a front one, and kept his keys in his hand.

"I'm going to go turn the room key in. I'll meet you at the truck." He left without waiting for a response.

So that's how it's going to be. She could live with that. They had a few hours left to endure each other's company, then she'd spell him to forget her and he'd be none the wiser. She could get through this.

The truck unlocked as she approached it, telling her Aidan was watching from the motel office. *Well, I'll show him.* She opened the passenger door, tossed her bag in first, and then attempted to leap in.

That was a big fail.

She tried jumping, grasping for the "oh shit bar," but his truck was just too damn tall. *What the hell does anyone need huge monster truck wheels for anyway?*

Before she could try again, she felt a tap on her shoulder. She turned to see Aidan, his face blank and unamused. He crouched, interlacing his fingers together to create a step for her, and nodded his head for her to go for it.

"Thanks." She stepped into his offered boost, using his shoulder to steady her as she scrambled into the truck.

He shut the door, saving her the embarrassment of trying to reach it.

They said nothing to each other on the way to the fast-food place. When he pulled up to the speaker and turned off the truck, he asked her what she wanted without sparing a glance in her direction. He accepted her money to pay for her own food this time, and then they traveled in almost virtual silence. From time to time she caught him side-eyeing her, his mouth opening and closing as if he wanted to speak but couldn't find the words, but he never managed to get it out.

As the road signs displayed smaller and smaller miles to their destination, a stupid desire to come clean and explain everything to Aidan built up in Sophia. But what would she say? *Oh, by the way, I'm a witch, and I've cast a spell on you. When it wears off, want to go for coffee and then some nookie if we learn that, in fact, your desire for me is real? But, oh, just so you know, it can never go any further than great sex because my coven frowns upon fraternizing with normal humans such as yourself.*

Even in her head it sounded crazy. No, she needed to stick to her original plan. In just a little while, he would leave, and—because of the spell of forgetfulness she'd cast—he'd never even remember he'd met her. The prospect did not cheer her.

By the time they finally pulled into the parking lot for the Covenhouse Inn, Sophia, so eager to get here when she'd started her trip what seemed like ages ago, wished they'd never arrived.

In a moment she would wipe Aidan's mind clean and send him on his way, never to cross paths again. She couldn't even visit him and pretend to meet him again for the first time to see how he was doing. To ensure he didn't remember, she had to steer clear of him forever. She lacked the skill to make her spell strong enough to withstand a test like that.

He'd go back to his life and the garage, with no memory of her, but she'd spend the rest of her life wondering *what if*.

What if I'd never cast the spell?

What if my broomstick hadn't broken down?

What if I'd never joined a coven that made me follow rules such as no relationships with humans?

The thing was, if she hadn't been in the coven, she wouldn't have learned witchcraft. She wouldn't have been able to spell a broom, and she wouldn't have broken down right near Aidan's garage. Why did it seem like every step she'd taken in life had led her to him, but for what?

Maybe with enough time, I'll be able to forget him, too.

"So, how long is this party thing going to last? Should I wait for you?"

Sophia swallowed hard as a vision of him nearly naked and lounging on hotel room sheets filled her mind. Heat rushed through her, which made her cheeks blossom with color.

With an almost inaudible growl, he leaned over and kissed her hard.

Sophia allowed it for a moment, and the fire and urgency his lips imparted made her regret even more keenly what she had to do. She pulled back before she could change her mind. She opened the door then turned sideways and slid out of the truck, letting herself fall down the last little bit and then stumbling a little when her feet finally hit the pavement. He leaned over the seat and stared down at her, questions in his eyes. This close it was an easy matter for her to mutter the words to the spell, sadness tainting the energy she formed and shaped into a pattern of forgetfulness. She flung the result at him.

His eyes widened, and in a rush, she spoke. "You will forget ever meeting me. Last night, after closing up, you felt the urge to go for a drive. You went farther than expected. But now you need to go home, back to your life, and forget you ever met me." His eyes clouded with hurt then confusion. She bit her lip in an attempt to not cry, not understanding why this affected her so. She whirled and walked away, her steps heavy and her heart a dead weight in her chest.

A part of her hoped she'd failed in her spell and

that, at any moment, she would feel his hands on her, spinning her around to tell her magic would never make him forget. Instead, the heavy rumble of his truck engine filled the air, a sound that receded as he drove away from her.

Blinded by tears, she told herself it was for the best. *A human and a witch—it would have never worked. But, oh, how I wish things could have been different.*

AIDAN CURSED as he drove away from the Covenhouse Inn. Sophia had blatantly rejected him. Sent him on his way as if he meant nothing. His *mate*. The woman he was supposed to spend the rest of his life with. Why would fate allow this to happen?

Perhaps he was wrong about it all. Maybe he'd jumped to conclusions too quickly. Was she not his mate? His wolf growled in his mind. *No, I'm not wrong. She is mine.* But what had just happened then? Did she not feel the same magnetic draw?

Too pissed off to pay attention to the road, he pulled over a few miles away and thought. He'd never learned why she'd gotten so upset when he tried to pleasure her the night before. A few times he'd thought about asking, but he didn't, opting instead to wait until she felt like bringing up the topic herself. Which, she never did.

What caused her hysterics? She'd wanted his touch —there was no denying it—yet she'd acted so strange.

Afraid. Maybe even guilty. Like what they were doing was *wrong* somehow. Why would that be?

Could she possibly have a man already back home?

Aidan's wolf side growled menacingly, angry at the thought, but the idea bothered Aidan's human side even more. *She is mine. I will allow no other to touch her.*

As he let his mind work over the few facts he had, it occurred to him that she had to be single. She didn't have the scent of another man clinging to her, and surely a lover would have at least kissed her goodbye, leaving a hint of a relationship on her skin.

Then what had made her reject him last night and again today? She hadn't been unaffected by their parting. He'd let his hurt cloud his mind, but when he thought back on their last moment together, he could see her eyes swimming in tears. It had hurt her to cast whatever spell she'd attempted to sling at him and to order him to leave and forget her. So why, then, did she do it?

He started to piece it all together, cursing himself for being an idiot. The biggest piece of the puzzle was simple: Sophia didn't know what he was. She thought him a mere human while she was a witch. If her coven was anything like his pack, humans, especially those privy to their secrets, were more than rare. She might have felt as if she had no choice but to send him away.

Then another realization hit.

I let her think I was a human under her control spell.

No wonder she'd reacted so poorly. Aidan slammed the steering wheel. "Fuck!"

He'd become so lost in his feelings for her and so focused on the realization that she was his mate, that he'd forgotten all about the fact that he'd acted as though her little spell had worked to compel him to drive her. She hadn't wanted to take advantage of him in bed, because she'd felt guilty for using him for a ride already.

Wait, what if the spell wasn't just to make him drive her? Was it supposed to control him in more ways than that? Did she think that he wasn't under his own control until she'd cast that final spell when he dropped her off?

He looked in his rearview mirror, down the road leading back to his mate. "I think we have a few things to clear up, sweetheart."

Like it or not, she was his. He'd let her have her little celebration for Halloween. However, he'd be nearby, ready and waiting, and once the gathering finished he'd reveal to her that she'd never been the one giving the orders. Then, they could finally give in to their destined pleasures.

At some point, he'd figure out how to share the truth of what he was and what she meant to him, and they'd need to figure out what they'd do about a pack and a coven that didn't approve of their union.

But not before we show each other how intense a true mate pairing could be.

6

Sophia should have gone downstairs to mingle with the others, but instead, she was in her room, alternately napping, crying, or pacing. Her mind spun as she waited for evening to fully fall, when she'd have to descend and join her coven sisters for the official festivities. She tried to regain her excitement over her first Samhain gathering as a witch. The exhilaration she'd basked in just days ago when the invitation arrived in the mail had vanished. Now, instead, all she could think of was Aidan, his last look of pain carving a wound into her heart.

I knew him for only a day. Not even. How could I have come to care for him so much in such a short time? She kept wondering what she could have done differently. How she could have kept him with her. However, everything revolved back to one simple fact. *He's human, and I'm not anymore.*

Sophia hadn't even known of her witchy heritage

until a few years back. Her parents had adopted her when she was still a baby, found supposedly abandoned. Her birth parents remained unknown even to this day.

She'd always known she wasn't the same as others. As a young child, Sophia had wondered if something was wrong with her because she'd always seen the world differently, a fact she learned to keep quiet about when her adopted mother dragged her to countless psychiatrists looking for a cure. She stopped telling people about how she could sometimes see colors swirling around her and touch those invisible streamers. She sealed her lips shut, not mentioning the ghosts she saw, along with other odd creatures like the gremlin that lived in her dad's garage. Silence was preferable to the strange looks and drugs prescribed by doctors who thought she suffered from a mental issue.

At the late age of sixteen when she finally began her menses, her otherworldly sense went into overdrive. Sophia feigned ignorance, even as her mother called in the priest to rid the house of the poltergeists. The only ghosts, though, were Sophia's awakening power, which manifested itself in floating objects and odd incidents.

Desperate to understand what was wrong with her and reassure herself she wasn't crazy, she went online, searching for her symptoms. She never found anything, but eventually, someone found her. Apparently, witches had embraced the technological age because her searches sent a red flag to the mother house, and in the dark of night, Sophia suddenly found herself abducted and given a lengthy interrogation, followed by a set of tasks, where, finally, her special abilities came into play.

When they'd told her she was a full-blood witch, one whose special parents had perished, Sophia laughed. Once the shock—and mirth—wore off, she was pleased to know she was normal, for a witch, at least.

Thus had begun her lessons. As an older student, one who hadn't been raised with an awareness of the magical world, she'd struggled. She needed to work harder than all the others to catch up to those who'd grown up in the lore—the varied rules and protocols adopted to keep them safe from humans. The Salem trials, which had seen countless innocents killed, served as an example of intolerance, one that, even today, served as a brutal reminder that safety lay in secrecy, or so the coven thought. Personally, she thought the modern world could handle the idea of witches, but one junior witch wasn't about to change hundreds of years of doctrine.

Along with history, spells, and witch law, another thing they'd taught her was, while she could dally sexually with humans, her kind avoided entering into permanent bonds with them. Not only were they forbidden to reveal their witch nature to humans—even spouses, which really complicated a marriage—but they also had to take into account that they would outlive their paramour. Part of being a witch meant a longer lifespan—two hundred years or more wasn't unheard of.

Sure, it wasn't exactly *forbidden* to intermarry, but the warning was clear. The most a witch could hope for was ten to fifteen years before she had to disappear, for the lack of aging eventually became noticeable and raised questions. Witches who refused to leave ended up finding their partners and children gone one day. Talk about an incentive to look at their kind first.

So really, sending Aidan away meant she'd saved him future heartache, and ensured he'd never become a target of some secret witchy cabal. Knowing this made Sophia's painful decision to let Aidan go seem noble, even if she didn't understand why she wanted him so much. She did know she didn't want to see Aidan hurt. He deserved a real life with a woman who could give him children and grow old with him. Not someone who would be forced to abandon him and their children within a decade or so.

But how she wished things were different. If only Aidan were one of the special folk allowed to know their secrets—elf, angel, demon, shifter, merman. So many species were allowed to know about her witch status, and, although not approved of for marriage—not that it stopped some—sexual dalliances were not uncommon.

Of course, that brought her back to the very core of it all, though. Aidan wasn't a man who could make his own choice in the matter. He was a human bespelled by a witch, and she'd never know what might have happened between them had she not cast on him. There was no reason to even consider giving up her spot in the coven, throwing it all away to be with him, because she didn't truly know if he liked her. Even if his lust was pure, and not just a side-effect of her spell, that didn't mean he wanted anything long-term with her.

The time for introspection passed. As the midnight hour approached, Sophia composed herself and left her room in her flowing robe, joining a chattering stream of witches out into the night. Lanterns lit the night sky and hung on branches and poles, illuminating their way to the gathering spot.

The Covenhouse Inn sat on over a hundred acres, ensuring the witches' privacy for ceremonies such as the one for Samhain. Most of the land was wooded, but as Sophia followed others of her kind through the meandering paths in the shadowy forest, it wasn't long before they emerged in a clearing with trampled grass. In the center of the huge space, a bonfire snapped and crackled, the flames licking up into the sky and popping with colors not usually seen—gold, red, purple, blue, and even some green. This close to the witching hour, power sizzled visibly all around her in a kaleidoscope of color. Excitement hummed in the air.

The witches stood shoulder widths apart and formed circles radiating outward from the fire. Sophia stood in one of the outer rings, her face tilted up to the sky as she stared at the fat, bright moon hanging over the assembly.

As if silenced by a spell, an instant quiet fell upon the clearing, and the chattering and rustling of hundreds of women was gone as expectancy hung heavy in the air.

Midnight hit unmistakably as the magical energy imbuing the world peaked. Samhain had arrived, with the power of its arrival zipping through her body like a lightning bolt. As if the fire and magic called them, ghostly forms rose in a sinuous trail from the bright flames, weaving and bobbing over the congregation. Like a signal, the dance began.

Unlike the Wiccans with their earth-based magic, Sophia belonged to a darker sect, one that still worshipped the Lord of Hades—with powerful results. Over the centuries, legends and rumors abounded about witches dancing naked around fires for Satan. Although never actually witnessed by human eyes—or at least no people who ever lived after seeing it—it was actually true. Liberating in so many ways, the dance brought them back to a primal time when witches were celebrated instead of persecuted. In a graceful move synchronized without practice, robes went flying off, which bared hundreds of females of all shapes and sizes. Male witches, also called *warlocks*, celebrated elsewhere in their own fashion.

Sophia vaguely felt the kiss of the cool night air on her naked skin. However, caught up in the building magic of the dance, she ignored it. Her body moved intuitively, weaving and swaying to an unheard rhythm, which made the gathered coven move in an undulating wave of bare skin and flying hair. Women of all ages and races spun faster and faster, their breath coming short, eyes gleaming, limbs flying.

Closing her eyes while opening her arms wide, Sophia basked in the power flowing throughout the clearing and felt her cares slip free. She lost herself in the wildness of the dance and twirled.

AIDAN RETURNED, and though he'd wanted to charge in to find Sophia and divulge the truth of what he was, he held back. Even with his limited knowledge of witches, he'd heard of this sort of gathering and understood the gravity of it. His pack had its own special events that weren't open to outsiders, and he could only imagine the pain the witches could inflict on him for interrupting a sacred celebration. No matter. He could wait to talk to Sophia, but that didn't mean that he would leave her alone. A protective instinct forced him to shift into his wolf form and wait, hidden, outside the inn until she appeared. His heart leaped at the sight of his witch in her ceremonial robes, and he double downed on his intention to follow her from a distance. Not that he expected trouble, but he liked to be prepared.

Oddly enough, when Aidan settled in a location with a good view of the bonfire, he found himself only one of several other shifters out in the woods that night. All were hidden, but he could sense and smell them. Some wolves, like himself, and other beasts as well—bear, panther, and even the musty scent of something akin to reptile. At first, his hackles rose, his instincts to protect his mate at the ready, and he prepared himself for a fight. But the more he scented and waited for the others to make a move, the more he realized that there was nothing malicious in the air. It seemed the others were there to observe, just as he was.

Satisfied they didn't present a danger, Aidan didn't ponder for long on the other shifters. He watched the witches pour into the open space, though his gaze remained trained on one body only—Sophia's. She looked pensive compared to the other happy, chattering witches, and he wondered—hoped—it was because she thought of him.

The fur on his body stood on end when a sudden silence overcame the group. Energy churned and boiled in the air, the result of having so many witches in one place and on such a powerful date. With an almost ecstatic burst, the magic overflowed to stroke everyone, including him, and left those in its wake feeling more alive than ever.

Aidan, who'd never heard of such a thing, howled in response, a sound repeated in different cadences all around the gathered women. He howled again when he saw Sophia shed her robe, her beautiful naked body moving sinuously as she danced alongside her sisters. Aidan in wolf form cried out again, unable to help himself as Sophia twirled faster and faster, perspiration gleaming on her bare skin, her hair twirling in a silken mess.

After several revolutions around the clearing, Sophia's face finally broke into an exhilarated smile, and with his enhanced hearing, he could pick out her melodic laughter among the others. It rang with joy, an emotion and sound repeated all over the place as the witches basked in the heady magic eddying around them.

Sophia was a radiant site. A witch in her element. His pagan mate, whose enjoyment in the dance stirred his lust.

The witches didn't seem to pay attention to the fire in the center, which became brighter and brighter the faster they danced, but stayed aware, even with his attention mostly captivated by Sophia. The flames seemed to have a life of their own, thriving off the energy of the coven. He alternated glances from Sophia to the fire, so he saw when a figure arose from the flames. A naked, solidly built man.

At the stranger's appearance, the witches, like puppets, collapsed to their hands and knees as if an unseen power had cut the strings that held them up. Kneeling on the ground, the witches swayed and hummed as they faced the man who still floated in the flames.

"My beautiful harem," boomed the man Aidan somehow instinctively knew was Lucifer. "Happy Samhain!"

"Lord of Darkness. Father of Sin. Satan love us. Lucifer bless us."

The pagan chant shocked Aidan. Another of the few facts he knew about witches, some were natural hippies—Wiccans—and the others were considered dark ones, and were said to worship the Devil.

Figures my true mate would be among the later. Not that he actually cared. Actions meant more than who you owed allegiance to. As a wolf, he and his pack worshipped no deity, even if they were aware and had a healthy respect for the superpowers known as God and the Devil.

Respect or not, Satan's next words made Aidan's vision turn red, and he growled.

"Who will serve their master tonight?" Lucifer dropped his hand to an engorged cock that put every mortal man to shame. "I have a mighty need to bless my flock."

Aidan went to lunge forward when Sophia stood, but he remained caught in place when a firm grasp took hold of his wolf's nape. He snarled, turning his head to bite at the intruder.

"Quiet, wolf," said a voice low in timbre but resonant with power.

In the darkness, Aidan couldn't make out the features of the human who held him, but inhaling, he noted the scent of reptile. *How the hell did he sneak up on me? Surely, I wasn't that distracted?* Evidently, he had been.

When Aidan quieted and relaxed, looking back to

the group of witches, the voice chuckled. "A wise decision. Not so smart, though, would be to interrupt what goes on in the field. Fear not, your lady has chosen to abstain from the festivities. Most witches who've found their mate do."

Indeed, Sophia had picked up a robe off the ground and shrugged it on before joining other robed witches in conversation a bit away from the fire. On the opposite side of the bonfire, several handfuls of witches joined the Devil in a naked orgy that Aidan found acrobatically impressive. Satan certainly was a skilled lover judging by the blurring motions and moans of the ladies as he managed to pleasure the large group.

Unable to speak to the man in beast form, Aidan shifted back, uncaring of his nakedness, a trait common among shifters who often found themselves without clothes. "She's not mine yet."

"Aah, just found her, did you?" Again, a chuckle floated from the darkness, and try as Aidan might with his enhanced eyesight, he could not see the shifter who spoke to him, almost as if the man could cloak himself in shadows.

"She doesn't even know what I am," Aidan muttered, keeping his eyes on the clearing, ensuring Sophia didn't escape his sight.

"Oh." The man's previously jovial tone turned somber. "Are you holding back because your pack leader refuses to approve of your union?"

"There's been no time to ask, yet." Usually, Aidan

wasn't the type to confide in strangers, but it seemed this man might have some insight into their situation, and he could take all the information he could get. "I know it's not common, but I don't see why there would be an issue. She's my true mate."

"The doubt in your voice tells me you're wiser than that. True mate or not, it will really depend on your pack alpha. Some actually welcome witches as mates, nowadays. They can make valuable additions to the pack. But then, there are others obsessed with the purity of the line."

Aidan pictured Jason, his alpha. A man just in his forties, yet still stubbornly stuck in the past. It wouldn't be easy to convince him. Suddenly, resentment alit in Aidan. Why was this stranger forcing him to think about all this, when he'd not even had a chance to talk it over with Sophia?

"Who the fuck are you, and why are you telling me all this? Why do you care?"

"My name is Dracin." He spoke calmly, unaffected by Aidan's tone. "Let's just say I know the interspecies mating thing can be an issue, and I thought I'd offer some advice, one shifter mated to a witch to another."

"*What* are you?" Aidan asked, taking another deep breath of the air to try once again to understand the man talking to him. "If I didn't know better, I'd say large reptile."

A chuckle came with a surprising answer. "I am a dragon."

"They don't exist." At least, that's what he'd always been told.

"Guess again." Amusement tinged Dracin's voice before the shadowy figure shrugged. "Now, you can take my advice or leave it. I don't really care. I just thought you might like a head's-up."

Aidan could sense no deception in his words, but he still didn't completely trust him. Dracin had, however, made the situation seem all that much more real to him. It was good to know that there were other interspecies pairs out there—not just that they existed, but that they were willing to help.

"I'm sure everything will be fine." Aidan couldn't hide his doubt completely.

"For your sake, I hope it is. However, should you find yourself cast out of the pack, tell your female to contact Clarabelle. My mate can give her directions to a pack that welcomes mixed pairings."

The shadowy Dracin began to retreat but Aidan stopped him, not wanting to lose a contact that might be able to help him as he pursued his destiny with a witch. "Wait. I have questions."

Dracin paused. "They'll have to wait for another time. Now, I must get to my witch and help her expend all the Samhain energy she's accrued tonight. You'll also want to catch up to yours. Fear not, though. I'll find you again when the time calls for it."

The stranger melted into the forest as mysteriously as he'd arrived, which left Aidan with a mind whirling with unknowns. His musings would have to wait. He didn't want to lose sight of Sophia, and she'd just started toward the path that left the clearing.

He changed back to his wolf form and then flitted through the trees, coming as close as he dared to the path, his keen nose picking up the unmistakably sweet scent of his soon-to-be forever mate. The stronger her scent became, the lighter his heart felt. *This is all going to work out. There's a group of shifters and witches, a whole pack that accepts our kind. Surely my pack will accept her, too.*

It was time to bring Sophia in on his plan. When he finally caught up to her, she was alone. *There's no time like the present.* He trotted out onto the path a few paces ahead of her and turned to face his beautiful mate.

He had a moment to see her eyes widen before she let out a piercing shriek.

Oops. Maybe not such a good idea.

7

Sophia recovered quickly from her fright when she realized the beast in front of her was only a wolf and not a demon. A wolf she could handle, especially since he wasn't snarling or growling or bearing his teeth. Though his size did intimidate, his bright green eyes seemed somehow familiar.

"Shoo, you overgrown mutt," she said as she waved her hands. She could have sworn the wolf's eyes rolled in mirth, and instead of leaving, it sat on its haunches, proudly displaying its black fur that seemed to reflect blue in the moonlight.

Well, that wouldn't do. She wasn't stupid enough to try and walk around it, becoming an easy target by getting too near or turning her back. Her body still thrummed with magic from the ceremony, so it was a simple matter to pull some into her palm to flick at the wolf, intending to sting it on the nose and send it scampering.

The power, however, when it came in contact with the shaggy beast didn't even startle it, and now the fear came creeping back. *What kind of wild creature is this that my magic doesn't affect?* Her magical annals never covered something like this.

They *did* cover the fact that shapeshifters had an immunity to magic, a fact she remembered when the hairy wolf's form began to shimmer and another shape began pushing through.

Crap!

Not waiting to wait around and see the wolf's full transformation, Sophia whirled and ran, her only thought being to get to the other witches as quick as she could, and knowing she was still closer to the clearing than the inn, she went in that direction. Hopefully some more senior witches—or the Devil himself!—could help her with more powerful magic.

She didn't get far before steel-band-like arms wrapped around her midsection and lifted her, which left her feet pedaling in midair. That didn't stop her from kicking and thrashing. "Let me go! You don't know who you are messing with."

"Oh, I know exactly who and what you are." A velvety and familiar voice tickled her ear.

Sophia froze. "Aidan?" *Impossible. I spelled him to forget me and then watched him drive away.*

Where had he come from? And what of the wolf she'd just seen? The wolf that hadn't behaved as a wild beast, that hadn't been affected by her magic, and that she'd been sure was in the middle of a shape shift.

The lack of snarling and snapping brought a realization that hit Sophia like the slam of a sledgehammer. "You're the wolf!" she accused.

His arms loosened, and she whirled around to glare at the man she'd thought was human. Even her annoyance at his deception couldn't stop heat from spreading through her limbs. *He came back.* And there he stood, without a stitch of clothing!

Sophia's blush warmed her cheeks, and she made sure to keep her eyes trained on his face and not the wickedly tempting expanse of naked flesh standing within reach. Blame it on the heightened energy from the bonfire dance, but her body ached for him even more than before.

"You're right, I'm not human, I'm a shapeshifter."

"You lied to me."

"Says the witch who tried to control me with a spell." He rolled his eyes.

A declaration less explosive than his admission he was something she'd never imagined she would encounter. A real werewolf. A man capable of changing into a beast. She'd heard the tales, learned about them in her studies, but it had all sounded so outlandish she'd barely paid any attention.

"Aren't you going to say something?" he prodded.

"Sit."

He arched a brow. "Excuse me?"

"Guess you're not that well-trained. Does that mean you don't fetch either?" Speaking of fetching, why did he come back? Her magic hadn't worked on him, but still, what reason did he have to return for her? On that note, why had he gone along with her commandeering of him as a chauffeur in the first place?

"I fetch when the prize is worth it," he said in his low growly voice, taking a step towards her.

She stepped away and averted her gaze, not wanting to be tempted by his muscular naked body. "What are you doing here?"

"I came looking for you."

A statement to make her heart stutter while she studied the bark of the nearest tree. "Why?"

"For the same reason I drove you to that crazy ass meeting. Because I have to be with you. You're my mate."

Sophia's head snapped back toward him, and her mouth dropped open so wide she could have caught flies. She knew that word—again from what little she'd studied of shifters—and exactly what it meant. "No way."

"Yes, way." He smiled at her again, his teeth flashing white. "Now, do you mind if we go *discuss* this somewhere more comfortable?"

She could read the intention in his eyes, and her cleft moistened in response. She was already sexually charged, and only a breath away from telling him, "come and get it." As if sensing her arousal, the man flared his nostrils and his eyes seemed to glow in the darkness, the animal side of him becoming readily evident and reminding her that the strongest lesson on shifters had been *don't become involved with one.*

Sophia took another few steps back and shook her head. "I'm not going anywhere with you. I know about your kind. I know what mate means. You want to get me alone so you can bite me and make me your sex slave. Sorry, but I am so not doing that."

"Mmm. My sex slave, eh?" His wicked grin made her nipples tighten, and it took a lot of willpower not to tackle him and ravish his naked body. "You make it sound like such a bad thing."

He licked his lips. Willpower didn't stop her aroused sex from wetting and throbbing, wanting his touch. Talk about distracting.

"So, you don't deny you want to mark me?" She tried to keep her rational mind at the forefront, tugging on her anger, her indignation—anything to fight his erotic pull.

"Oh, I want to mark you all right, sweetheart, and not just with my teeth. But don't worry. When I do bite you, I promise you'll enjoy it."

"But I don't want you to." If she allowed it, she'd lose everything from her membership in the coven to her freedom. He'd have the ability to lock her up and throw away the key—and she'd be helpless to even fight against him.

"Your body says differently."

Sophia stamped her bare foot, grounding herself in the dirt and using it to steady her mind. "Lust has nothing to do with this. Sex is something I can walk away from. You forcefully binding me to you isn't. I won't allow it."

Aidan's face darkened. "So, I guess it was okay when you thought you'd spelled me and forced me to take you here?"

Sophia winced. "That was different. I used you for one day, and, yes, I admit it wasn't right. But what you're talking about is a heck of a lot longer—*forever*, right? So, the answer is no. Now go before I call my sisters." She ignored the little whisper in the back of her mind that suggested forever with Aidan might not be all that bad, and she started to run.

Only to immediately trip over an exposed root, and go sprawling onto the ground.

Aidan crouched down next to her, shaking his head. "Not exactly a daughter of the woods, are you?"

"Go away," she spat.

"I'll leave, but you're coming with me."

"Think again." Sophia opened her mouth to scream and call her sister witches for help, but he clamped a hand over her mouth. *You've got to be kidding me. How dare he!*

She bit him, hard, but he didn't even flinch. The sound of ripping fabric filled the air as he tore a strip from the sleeve of her robe, and a moment later, he stuffed his makeshift gag into her mouth and tied it in place. She pulled at it, but he'd tied it too tightly for her to rip it away. When she glared daggers at him, he just shrugged unapologetically.

"You'll thank me later."

Then the jerk hauled her off the ground and slung her over his shoulder. Initially, when her face brushed the naked—scorchingly lickable—skin of his back, she forgot to breathe. But common sense returned quickly, and she pummeled his bare back and kicked her feet. He responded with a firm whack to her bottom.

He spanked me! Enraged, she did all she could to fight against him, but several more resounding slaps on her ass later, she finally stilled. Not only had she not managed to even come close to escaping his iron grip, her ass now throbbed painfully. Even more disturbing, her pussy throbbed too. With pleasure.

Oh, I am going to make him pay when I get free. Angry words and intentions, and yet her body still betrayed her, pulsing with heat and arousal.

Don't get distracted *by her obvious arousal*. Not an easy feat given the perfume of her surrounded him, tempting him to dip his hand under her flimsy robe and stroke her wet core. His more primal side screamed for him to stop and toss her to the ground for a proper ravishing.

There will be plenty of time to ravish her later. First, let's get out of here before she brings a whole coven of witches on top of me and I learn exactly how much magic it takes to spell a shifter.

Aidan didn't plan to take her kicking and screaming, but what choice did he have when his mate flat-out refused him? It was only a matter of time before other witches wandered upon them and took Sophia's side on the matter. Usually a reasonably level-headed man, he lost his senses at the idea of being kept from her. He needed time to clear up her misunderstandings about shifters and mates, so he'd gagged her when she would have screamed her pretty face off and carried her, struggling like a hellcat, to where he'd parked his truck.

He'd be lying if he denied that he'd enjoyed smacking her full bottom, a practice he'd heard of but never partaken of before. He did note for future reference, though, the effectiveness of the punishment. Not only did she end up behaving, but her arousal thickened, spinning around him in a heavy perfume. His body clamored to seduce her, but so close to her sisters, he didn't dare.

He'd need to drive her away from the Covenhouse so he could work on helping her see that pairing up with him wouldn't be as horrible as she thought. *Sex slave indeed.* She didn't seem to realize that the intense desire she felt went both ways.

He made quick work of the distance between the woods and his truck, which he'd parked away from the inn on a deserted road. It amazed him actually that no other witches had come across them during their disagreement. *I wonder if my new friend, the dragon, played a part in that.*

He arrived at his truck, easily holding onto Sophia with one hand while he opened the passenger door with the other. He quickly placed her on the seat and shut her in, but as he rounded the truck, she jumped out.

In retrospect, he wasn't sure why he'd thought she would stay put.

He sensed more than heard her cry of pain as the little idiot hit the ground. He was immediately by her side, crouching in the gravel where she sat rubbing her ankle.

"This is your fault!" She'd finally managed to rid herself of the gag and was trying to shrivel him with a glare, but he shook his head at her.

"Stubborn witch, aren't you? Did you really think you were going to escape?"

"A girl's got to try," she said sulkily.

He chuckled at her spirit and then palpated her hurting ankle. His wolf, roused by the pain he could faintly feel emanating from her, paced in his mind unhappily. It stunned him that a mental resonance had already begun between him and Sophia, one that allowed him to sense some of her thoughts and emotions. It was a little disconcerting, especially the knowledge that their eventual mating would amplify it. A benefit or curse, depending on how you looked at it.

"Come on." With a sigh, he swung her into his arms and brought her back to the truck, perching her back on the seat with stern regarded. "Do I need to tie you to the dash, or are you going to sit there like a good little girl?"

"I can't exactly run away with a twisted ankle." She scowled at him and crossed her arms.

He arched a brow. "Look, I just want to talk, okay? I'm not going to bite you or do anything you don't ask for, alright? I'd just like you to give me some time to help you understand all this."

"I don't want to understand this. I want to forget I ever met you!"

The words stung, but he doubted she really meant it. "Do you?"

The glare she shot at him melted into resignation. "I think it would be easier if I could."

"It would be easier if you stopped fighting and just agreed to come with me."

With a large sigh, she relented. "I'll stay, for now."

He inwardly chucked at her stubborn nature, something he admired. He'd never imagined himself shackled to a weak-willed lily.

He rounded the other side and reached into the cab, pulling out clothes and dressing quickly. He loved the way she studiously ignored him, staring out her window instead of gracing him with even a sideways glance. He loved, even more, the scent of her arousal, which, even as angry as she was, she couldn't control.

He started the truck and pulled onto the road. Next stop, his cabin, where he'd have his work cut out for him if he wanted to convince her to let him claim her.

Ah, the pleasurable things a man's got to do for his woman.

8

Sophia kept her mouth shut and refused to look at Aidan. Part of her thought she should have attempted to run or scream again, but the other was glad she had a chance to be with him. She knew she should try to resist, but in the close confines of the cab, she couldn't help but notice the heat radiating from him. Her treacherous body replied in turn by moistening her cleft and tightening her nipples. Dressed in only her robes, she felt her thighs rub together slickly and her tight nipples protrude beneath the cloth. She chewed thoughtfully on her bottom lip. *I guess there's no denying, even with his caveman tactics, that I'm attracted to him. But, dammit, it's one thing to be attracted, a whole other to be his slave for the rest of my life.*

That was what mates were, right? She pressed her lips together, trying hard to remember what she'd learned about other beings. There were those who resembled humans, like shifters and the fey, and they'd spent a whole week on shifters. There were different classes divided into lupine, feline, ursine—more commonly known as bears—and aquatics.

The lupine—wolves—was what she needed to remember now. She recalled the fact that they lived in communities, families of other wolves, and those communities were called packs, where an alpha set the rules. Unlike portrayals in legends and movies, shapeshifting was not contagious but rather a matter of genetics.

She unfocused her eyes from the tree line so she could see Aidan in the reflection of the glass. Was this determined man the alpha of his pack? He seemed young to hold such a powerful position, but supposedly the position of pack leader was often based on strength. If that were the case, then Aidan definitely fit the bill. She certainly couldn't imagine him kowtowing to someone else. From the lesson he'd taught the man who'd tried to assault her in the diner, to the way he'd refused to give up on her just now in the woods, he'd proven just how stubborn and determined to do things his own way he was.

She shook her head, realizing how foolish she'd been. How could she have missed all the signs that he hadn't fallen for her persuasion spell? They were there. If she'd stopped feeling guilty and assuming she miscast the spell, she might have noticed that he wasn't as human as she'd assumed him to be.

She changed the direction of her thoughts, determined to retain control of her mind and body and not lose herself in the lusty aura Aidan had captured her in. Could shifters cast a kind of thrall on their targets? Was that what Aidan had done to her? Perhaps the whole time she'd thought he was acting out her innermost desires, he was actually putting some kind of mate spell on her.

As she sifted through the shifter knowledge that had been living dormant in her mind, more and more came back to her. Specifically about the mating aspect of their kind. Shifters bonded for life. No one was quite sure how the magic of it worked, but once the male marked his chosen one by biting her hard enough to draw blood, something happened. A twining of souls, some opined. Controlling magic, argued others. Whatever the underlying factor, the end result was unanimous—the pair became utterly devoted to each other.

Not too bad-sounding until you read further and found out that, while the men continued to live life as before, the women gave up everything and became noting more than their mate's sex chattel and *breeder,* as Sophia's teacher had sneeringly called them.

It was supposedly necessary for the women to be guarded closely—*protected,* some claimed, stripped of all freedoms, said others—if they were to ensure their lines. Under normal circumstances, pregnancies push a woman's body to great levels of stress and endurance, but a shifter fetus is stronger than a regular human baby. It takes even more effort to grow and nourish them, and they take a considerable toll on their mother. Because of such, packs have extremely high mortality rates. Her books claimed that the mate bond was there to ensure the women stayed tied to the hearth and avoided any extra risks or undue strain on their bodies while they give themselves to their mate and their future potential offspring.

Sophia continued to dig back into her memories of what she'd studied. Shapeshifters did occasionally breed outside their packs, but ran into difficulty as the whole interspecies thing came with decreased fertility odds. A non-shifter's body wasn't built to cope with a shifter fetus. Very rarely a shifter would be born of such coupling, but usually, the babes ended up being appalling... human.

So the textbooks said. The low incidences of this type of mating made information more difficult to come by because both sides tended to guard the purity of their bloodlines closely. Sophia hadn't even bothered to ask for elaboration in class, because it had never occurred to her that she'd be in the position herself. Since she'd not grown up in the magical community, she'd still been wrapping her mind around the fact that witches were real and so was the Devil. She hadn't any extra headspace to think that someday she'd meet a shifter—let alone fall for one.

Though, if she *had* bothered to ask, she would have been reminded that the coven greatly discouraged interspecies breeding because of the dwindling witch and warlock population. They were all encouraged to guarantee the continuation of their magical line by settling down with a warlock and having as many babies as possible.

Now that she thought about it, perhaps their coven's expectations weren't that much different than the shifter packs having what her teacher called *breeders*. It seemed both groups were driven to generate more of their kind.

Yet, this all didn't make complete sense to Sophia. Yes, settling down with another magic-user ensured that the progeny would inherit their sire and dame's magical abilities, but there were plenty of stories of witches who'd been born of a witch and non-magic user. Some offspring even had more powers than full-blooded witches.

Wait... there was something else.

"Witches who mate with shifters lose their magic," her teacher had said. *"The exact cause is unclear, though it's thought that the mating bite not only puts a witch into life-long service to the shifter, but also takes away the witch's power. Some have retained it, but the moment they become pregnant, it all vanishes."*

She'd lose her magic. That was it. The final straw. She'd always wanted to have children and a family of her own. Being an orphan adopted into a family of non-witches, she'd imagined what it would be like to have the perfect little magical family someday. But being with Aidan meant being used for sex, tempting death if she became pregnant with a shifter baby, and losing her magic—the thing that made her special.

Sophia took a steadying breath. There was a way

out of this. A quite simple one. All she needed to do was convince Aidan to pick someone else to be his mate, and he'd release her.

With the plan in mind, the darkness and the drive lulled her, and Sophia lost the struggle with her eyelids. She woke hours later to full daylight, only to discover her head nestled in his lap.

She scrambled upright, and her cheeks heated at his low chuckle. After scrubbing at her eyes, she looked around, not recognizing anything. The forest around the Covenhouse Inn hadn't been nearly as dense as this one, and the road now went up and down steep rolling hills.

She'd obviously slept a while since the sun seemed to have moved past midday.

"Where are we?"

"Close."

She pursed her lips at his oblique answer. "Close to where, smartass?"

"You'll see." With that enigmatic answer, he started to whistle jauntily while Sophia simmered.

Her stomach growled, and she wanted to die of embarrassment, but instead, she embraced anger. "So, does your convincing me to be your concubine include starvation?"

"Look behind your seat."

Sophia craned around and saw a cooler. Lifting the lid, she found cold water bottles, packaged sandwiches, and fruit. "Nice to know you came prepared for your kidnapping."

"Actually, I stopped while you were asleep."

"While I was asleep?" Something was fishy. "And I didn't wake up? In all these hours?" She peered at him suspiciously and was rewarded with color blooming on the tops of his cheeks.

"I might have had some help with that," he admitted. "I ran into a friend who offered to help by weaving a sleep spell around you to allow me to make it to our destination."

"A kidnapping accomplice," she accused.

"No!" He ran a frustrated hand through his hair. "It's not like that. He's someone I met while we were watching you witches dance."

"You mean you weren't the only one spying on us?" she asked as outrage filled her.

"What do you want me to say?" Aidan shrugged while a smile crept on his face, revealing his deep sexy dimple to her. "There were actually quite a few people in the words. Apparently, your celebration isn't just for witches."

"Did you enjoy the show?" she asked, unable to hide the jealous growl.

"Very much. Don't worry, though, you were by far the hottest witch there," he added, taking his eyes off the road to look at her directly with his mischievous smile. "I quite enjoyed the way you shook that luscious ass of yours and the way your tits jiggled. Maybe you can give me a private dance later?"

She looked away, opting to fish out food from the

cooler. "So, I dozed off and you stopped to let your newfound friend put a sleep spell on me."

"Yeah, when I stopped for gas, he was already there waiting for me, and before you ask me how, I don't know." As he said this, the road they were on went from pavement to packed dirt, and Sophia bounced and jiggled on her seat as he drove over the ruts.

She focused on eating instead of conversing. She wanted to feel angry he'd watched her, but instead, she fought two vastly different emotions. Arousal because his words made her picture herself giving him an up-close-and-personal dance wearing nothing. The other emotion made no sense. It felt like jealousy. The idea he'd laid eyes on other naked women did not please her at all. Yet why should she care? Didn't she *want* him to target someone else for his mate so she could be free?

It wasn't long before the bumpy road finally ended in a clearing, wherein a log cabin sat. *Rustic* didn't begin to describe the setting. When he parked, she stepped out, noting that they were surrounded by woods and the only sound she could hear was the ticking of the hot engine accompanied by bird calls. Sophia, a city girl at heart, didn't like it one bit.

Aidan rounded the truck and helped her out, standing her on her two feet. Only when she put pressure on her ankle did she remember her earlier injury, but to her surprise, she felt not a twinge. To test it, she walked around a few paces before whirling to eye him questioningly.

"What did you do?"

"Me? Nothing. Dracin healed you after he put the sleep spell on you."

"Dracin being the friend you made in the woods?"

He nodded. "He claimed dealing with a wounded witch would be worse than a wet cat who just had a bath."

Sophia snorted and turned back to face the log cabin. She marveled at its size and quaint rustic look. Despite the mortared and fitted logs, it had big, modern windows that faced out into the yard. A screen door hid the solid wood front door. Aidan carried in the cooler, among other things, leaving her alone outside.

She twirled to look for an escape and ended up sighing. *Welcome to the boonies. Maybe I can hitch a ride with a moose.* Escape on foot would require a great deal of walking, judging by how long they'd driven on the dirt path with no other signs of habitation. She doubted he had any neighbors in proximity she could turn to.

Aidan came back outside. "The nearest house is about a five-mile hike east, and if you're looking for the main road, it's southwest about seventeen clicks."

"As if I'd walk. I just need a broom."

"It's broke, but I think I have a feather duster you can try riding."

"I hate you."

"You just think you do because you're horny."

Sophia gaped at him. "I! Of all… I am not!"

"Don't worry, sweetheart, as soon as I get the woodstove ready for the night and the food put away, I'm going to take care of you."

Sophia shivered involuntarily at his words, and all her hormones screamed *yes* as they flooded her pussy with moisture. "You'll have to force me because I will not bed you willingly."

Aidan's face tightened, and his words emerged clipped. "I won't need to force you. You're going to beg me to take you. Hell, I can smell your body's desire from here already. So, anytime you're ready, just say please."

"I hate you!" she yelled at his retreating back as he took another load of stuff into the cabin.

"Love you, too, sweetheart."

Sophia stamped her foot, her frustration over the situation nothing compared with her annoyance at the warmth his words created. She didn't want to have all her freedoms taken away—to be locked up in a secluded cabin with a stranger, no matter how good the sex might be. She wanted to go home and forget she had ever met Aidan, even if he was more exciting than anyone else she'd ever met. If only he were a warlock and not a shifter who claimed she was his mate. She would have jumped all over him. Heck, if he hadn't stated his intention to bite her, she would have bedded him anyway. More than once, too.

But forever with a wolf? It would never work. Right?

TO DRIVE Sophia absolutely nuts and heighten the sexual tension he sensed building in her, Aidan ignored her. Not as easy as it sounded since the only thing he wanted to do was tear her robe off, bury his prick into her velvety wetness, and bite her as he pumped her fast and hard. It didn't help that his wolf refused to go to sleep, his furry presence growling and yipping demands in Aidan's mind.

Aidan was determined, though, to make her ask for it. Call it pride, call it preserving his skin, either way, he was determined to make her admit she wanted him, no matter what she said. He could smell her desire, and while he knew he could seduce her, he knew that method of his taking would always be a bone of contention. Not the most auspicious way to start their new life.

Hence, the plan he hatched on the drive to his remote cabin—the place where he escaped when he wanted a place he could be his furry self. He could smell her desire for him, see it in the way she watched him. If he turned it up a notch, he figured it would only be a matter of time until she caved to her desires. And by not mauling her right away, he'd give her a chance to get to know him, to ask questions, and to realize that her impression of shifter mating wasn't entirely accurate. She'd equated it with being a slave, and yet like any species, relationships differed from couple to couple. He couldn't deny some men treated their women like chattel whose only purpose was to serve and breed. Others, like Aidan, accepted them as equal partners and had expectations of the mating that included friendship and comradery perhaps even more than sex and breeding. Convincing Sophia of that would prove interesting.

For the moment, until she gave him a chance to show his true character, he'd play dirty. Food stored away and the windows opened to air out the place, as he hadn't been up in a few weeks, he prepared for round one in the seduction plan. Since she'd refused to enter the cabin, opting instead to take a seat outside on the back porch, he went that way, stripping off his shirt in front of her and then heading for the wood pile. Her gasp and heightened scent of arousal as he walked by without acknowledging her wasn't lost on him. His cock throbbed painfully behind the zipper of his jeans. He'd need a long, cold shower before the day was through, unless he managed to drive her mindless with arousal to the point that she jumped him. *Please.*

He picked up the ax and started to chop wood he didn't need, enjoying the pain and pleasure of the task. Pleasurable because with every swing that sent his muscles rippling, her desire ramped up a notch and her pheromones drifted to him in the air, but painful because, much as he wanted to fuck her, he knew she wouldn't give in to bliss so easily.

But once she did...

A good thing he had an axe to swing because he needed to do something to ease his tension.

9

Kidnapped and brought to a lonely cottage in the wood and what did the jerk do?

Chopped wood.

Shirtless.

Sophia's mouth went dry, even as her cleft became soaked. Aidan didn't seem to notice her as he worked, but, oh, how she noticed him. How could she not with his muscular torso rippling with each stroke? His naked skin glistening with sweat? Her eyes were riveted on the light trail of chest hair that led down in a *V* to his...

With a curse, she averted her gaze, her breath short. *Madness!* How could just simply looking at him make her want to throw caution to the wind and dive on him to molest his deliciously sinful body? Even now, facing away from him, her channel throbbed, aching for something thick and long and...

Cursing again, she strode into the cabin, the faint

sound of a chuckle following her. *Jerk.* He knew she wanted him, which frustrated her to no end. If only she could trust his promise to not bite her. Then maybe they could assuage their lust—several times—and then maybe he'd be willing to see that they weren't meant for forever-after.

The direction of her thoughts made her freeze as she paced inside. She'd not even been at the cabin an hour yet, but already she looked for ways to seduce him with no strings. He'd made it clear he could be ruthless in the pursuit of what he wanted. Look at his abduction of her. Who was to say a promise he wouldn't bite wouldn't be broken in the heat of the moment or when she was so consumed with passion she'd agree to anything? How could she know that his wolf side wouldn't take over and demand it? No, she needed to fight this attraction she had for him and, even more importantly, find a way to escape. *Soon, because I don't how long I can fight my own body. Even my heart sings when he's around.*

It was while she roamed his cabin restlessly that she came across her bag. *How the heck did he get his hands on it?* She'd left it locked in her room back at the inn. Did that stranger, Dracin, have something to do with it? Aidan had mentioned him enough for it to become clear the man was something of an accomplice in all of this.

Puzzled by its presence, but glad she could change out of the ceremonial robe, she armed herself in jeans and a shapeless sweatshirt. Then she pulled out her book and settled on the couch, determined to take her mind off the sexy lumberjack outside.

Eventually Aidan came inside, and with great force of will, she steadfastly refused to look up from her book. She only trembled slightly when she heard the sound of running water as he showered. *Don't think of him standing under the sluicing water, naked.* She bit her nails right down for the first time since her teens, when she'd kicked the nervous habit.

When he finally re-appeared, fully clothed—unfortunately—he still didn't speak to her, but when she looked up he did throw her a grin, which made her scowl. Even fully clothed and hiding the too-tempting sight of his upper body, he still caused a mounting arousal in her. She couldn't help but notice as the material stretched and hugged his hidden muscles, which just served to act as erotic enticement. Now she simply wanted to strip the shirt from him—with her teeth.

He chuckled and walked over to the kitchen area, moving around with ease while he set up a propane stove and pulled out steak and potatoes.

She didn't understand what game he played. When he'd told her she was his mate and he intended to claim her, she'd expected him to ravish her at the first moment he could. Or at least, work on wooing her. He hadn't—the jerk. Instead, he barely paid her any mind, going about his chores and not making any attempts to seduce her at all. It made a girl want to throw a dramatic fit, starting with taking off all her clothes. A naked witch in his living room would probably wipe that serene look off his face and get her the action she craved.

What the hell is wrong with me? I don't want to be claimed by a werewolf. Remember the long list of reasons why this is a horrible idea? So, why am I so miffed he's ignoring me?

She jumped when he finally spoke. "How do you like your sausage?"

Erect and in my sex were the first words that came to mind, but what she said was, "You pig! I told you I wouldn't sleep with you."

Aidan quirked a brow at her and shook his head. "I was just asking how you liked your breakfast sausage, sweetheart. For tomorrow morning's breakfast. What a dirty mind you have, though. I like it."

Sophia blushed crimson and didn't reply.

"Come and have some supper. You must be hungry."

She sure was, but stomach hunger fell second to the lusty hunger that dominated her thoughts. The worst part? She could have exactly what her heart desired if she just said the word. In a refusal to feed *that* appetite, Sophia slid into a wooden chair at the small table, where he'd placed two steaming plates of fried potatoes, steaks looking perfectly seared, and even side salads. It would figure he'd also know how to cook.

"I figured from the way you ate at the diner that you'd be a steak and potatoes girl."

He wasn't wrong, but Sophia didn't stroke his ego over it. She concentrated on eating. However, no matter how much food she swallowed, her other hunger didn't abate. She wanted something else to devour, she wanted to be freed from the carnal torment, and she knew all she had to do was say the word, and he'd give her dessert.

The silence stretched between them, taut as a strung wire, and Sophia almost snapped with the tension. "Why are you doing this?"

"Doing what?"

Sophia made a frustrated sound. "This! Bringing me here and then ignoring me. I'm not going to change my mind."

"And neither will I," he said flatly. "I don't know why you keep choosing to deny the connection between us, the rapport. Have you so quickly forgotten the trip to the inn before you knew what I was? Have you forgotten everything we had in common, how well we got along?"

Sophia looked down at her plate, where she absently twirled her fork in the leftover food. "It was different then."

"Why?"

"Because then you weren't trying to make me into your slave."

"No. But you'd thought that you'd successfully cast a spell to make me *yours*."

"That's different!" She objected, dropping her fork and sitting up straight to look him in the eyes.

"How?" He raised a brow.

"It was temporary," she sputtered, trying to rationalize it to herself as well as him. "I needed a ride, and yes, I took advantage. I felt guilty the whole time, but we're talking about a few hours and some gas—"

"And a hotel. And food."

She shook her head in frustration. "Fine, gas, hotel, food—but I'd left money in your glove compartment to pay you back."

"What about my time?" He sat back in his chair, crossing his arms and running his tongue over his bottom lip. "You didn't know if I had work or not the next day. Did you think about how I could have lost my job if I'd been a no-show because I was off carting your ass around?"

"You own the garage with your brother," she pointed out, though her voice came out softer as the idea sank in.

"You didn't know that when you targeted me to be your unwilling chauffeur."

"It's still not the same." She cleared her throat, determined to regain her confidence as she argued against his mating. "I borrowed you for one day, and I'm sorry for it, but you're wanting to enslave me for *life*."

"Stop using that word." Aidan slapped his hands down on the table, and Sophia jumped. "Mating is not about ownership. It's about two beings meant to come together. About sharing their life and love."

"Love?" Sophia laughed bitterly. "Oh, please. You

don't love me. We've barely known each other for two days."

"And?" He leaned forward and reached across the table, taking her hand in his. "Are you going to deny you didn't want me from the first moment you saw me? I know I wanted you."

"That's lust," she retorted, averting her gaze from his eyes that pled with her. "Not love."

"Semantics. Most relationships start with lust and evolve into love."

"And sometimes, after the lust has faded, there's nothing left, not even like." She tried to tug her hand away from his, but his grip held firm. "How can you be so sure that won't happen?"

"Because I have faith."

Still looking away from him, Sophia snorted. "That seems awfully risky."

"Love is risky, no matter what." His thumb grazed over her wrist where her quick pulse betrayed her feelings, and she finally managed to wrench away from his grasp.

"Sorry, but I don't think I'm ready to make that kind of commitment, especially knowing the repercussions." She looked back at him, wanting him to understand how serious she was.

"Like what? More pleasure than you can imagine?" The sweet look in his eyes steeled to passion, and his words made her shiver. She knew he spoke the truth when he promised pleasure, but pleasure was fleeting.

"Stop doing that. You know what I'm talking about. The side effects of a witch mating with a shifter."

His brows furrowed and he gave her a slight head shake. "I've never heard of any so-called side effects. Then again, I've never actually met a witch-and-shifter pairing. Dracin didn't have time to tell me much about his relationship."

"Why do you think there's so little shared about these pairings? Have you considered that?"

"They're not often allowed," he replied with a shrug. "I didn't really know they happened at all until I spoke with Dracin."

"Then maybe you should do a little more research." She looked down at her hands as she twisted them in worry. "What little I learned in my witch classes point out basic physical incompatibilities."

"Such as?" He gestured with his hand for her to continue.

"Well, such as the fact that shifter offspring are harder for non-shifters to carry. If we were able to conceive at all, it wouldn't be likely that my children would be magical like me."

"You're already thinking about our kids?" he teased, much to her frustration.

"You don't get it, do you? Non-shifters who get pregnant with shifter offspring have a higher chance of *dying* because their bodies aren't built to sustain the strong fetus."

"Oh." The jovial look melted from his face. Smug as that made her feel, she didn't stop with her tirade.

"And if I *were* to successfully carry our offspring, it would be at the price of losing my magic."

His eyes blinked in shock as he processed her words, and his tongue ran over his lips. Before speaking, he took a deep breath. "I assume this knowledge is based in fact and not rumor?"

Sophia frowned at him. "Why would they teach it to us if it were false?"

Aidan's mouth twisted into a grim frown. "Is it a permanent loss of magic, or temporary? Shifter females can't transform while pregnant, but they get it back after five months."

"Five months?"

"The length of their pregnancy. Shifter babies don't take as long as human babies to mature."

"Oh." The books hadn't mentioned that, not that it mattered.

"Besides, I didn't bring you here to make you pregnant. I brought you here for you to see that it's worth giving me a chance. I want to mate with you. To have a possible future with you, and while I always figured there would be kids, maybe there won't be. Would that be so bad?"

"Yes!" Sophia cried out without thinking. "Maybe that's easy for you to give up on the idea of a family, but I grew up without any blood relations. I grew up thinking I was odd. Ever since I found out I was a witch, I've pictured what it might be like to have my own little magical children. And then some stranger swoops out of nowhere and decides to steal all that away from me?" Tears prickled her eyes, though she hadn't expected to become so emotional.

"I didn't know."

"Of course you didn't," Sophia tried to steady herself. "We both know so little. We don't even know if it's pregnancy that takes away my magic, or if it will happen with your mating bite."

"I refuse to believe that's true," he said stubbornly. "It couldn't be, not with so many shifters out in the woods watching their mates dance around the fire. No way that many witches would have mated and lost their power and it not been known to you and the others."

"I can't risk it." His logic may have been sound, but not sound enough for her to risk it all. "We hardly know each other at all. What I *do* know? That my magic is a part of who I am. That people like you and I have enemies, and I need my magic to survive in this world."

A darkness entered Aidan's eyes. He rose from his chair, his body taut, and pulled her up into his arms. In shock from the multitude of pleasurable sensations racing through her, Sophia didn't protest. She did, however, shiver at his next words.

"I will never allow anybody or anything to hurt you. I will protect you with my life."

Then his mouth came down hard on hers.

10

AIDAN HONESTLY HADN'T INTENDED TO KISS SOPHIA. He'd meant to make her think about some of her arguments and then go to bed, but when she'd talked about needing magic to keep herself from harm, a raging protective instinct had taken over. Only a fool would dare to lay a finger on her. He would kill to keep her safe.

He'd meant only to reassure her when he pulled her into his arms, but his libido took over and his mouth claimed hers in a fiery kiss. With an expectation that she'd bite his lip or stomp on his insole, he was surprised when, instead, he felt her hands reach up to clutch at his head, drawing him down farther so that she might return his embrace with an enthusiastic groan.

She was everything he'd ever dreamed of in a woman—stubborn, intelligent, passionate, and, even better, fit perfectly against him. Her curvy frame tucked into his as if made for size. Her full breasts pushed against his chest, her rounded ass filled the palms of his hands lusciously, and her sex pulsed against the thigh he inserted between her legs.

Her mouth parted under the pressure of his, and he inserted his tongue into her warm recess, almost losing control when she daringly sent her tongue to twine with his. The heady sensations that swirled through his body were unlike anything he'd ever experienced. And he wanted more.

As he gripped her buttocks, he slid her up and down on his muscled thigh and was rewarded with a gasp, whose sound he swallowed. Even through the thickness of the clothes that separated them—he'd almost chuckled at her attempt to hide her shape under her bulky sweatshirt—she was so wet and ready for him. His lips left hers to taste the soft skin of her neck, and here his wolf finally jumped in, forcing his canines down and ramping up his instinct to bite her. *Mark her as mine.*

But an ounce of sanity prevailed. *She hasn't agreed yet.*

Cursing himself for being an idiot, but knowing he'd be stupider to go on without her permission, he pulled away from her and took a step back.

She swayed on her feet, with her eyes closed dreamily and her lips swelled with passion. She mewled like a lost kitten, and he took another step back, even as his wolf and heart screamed at him to scoop her up and take her now.

Finally, she opened her eyes, confusion quickly clearing. A red stain bloomed across her cheeks, and a torrent of emotions crossed her face. Before she could speak, Aidan did.

"There are blankets in the closet if you want some. I'll be in the bed if you change your mind about becoming my mate—or if you just want to cuddle. Goodnight."

Then he walked away from her, his cock and his wolf howling in protest. But Aidan knew he'd done the right thing. *It won't be long before she comes to me.*

HE WALKED AWAY. Sophia stared incredulously at his retreating back, not snapping out of her shock until he closed the bedroom door. She should be glad he'd walked away. She certainly hadn't given it a thought once he touched her. On the contrary, she wanted to stalk across the cabin into the room he'd vanished into and demand he finish what he'd started.

Her pussy throbbed, her nipples ached, and a frustrated moan broke free. She kicked and stamped at the floor, pissed at the effect he'd so easily wrought. *I'm even angrier at the fact that I want him to come back and continue where he left off.*

She tried to work the sexual frustration off by

cleaning up their dishes, but it did little to stop her mind from whirling with thoughts of a potential union. Even as she'd argued with him why their getting hitched wouldn't work, she'd heard her explanations for what they were—feeble excuses. So what if she didn't birth biological children? The thought alone gave her a painful stab to the heart, but she knew that many women—human, witch, and shifter alike—dealt with infertility. It was painful, and it took a lot of strength to live through it, but it was possible. Plus, as someone raised by adoptive parents, she knew very well that there were children in need out there who she could take in and love just as fiercely as any others. Maybe there were even children with magical abilities who needed her as much as she needed them.

She sighed. She was getting ahead of herself. Aidan had raised a good point: what if what she'd been taught was wrong? What if there *were* ways they could have children? What if having children didn't take away her power forever?

There must be ways for a mating between a witch and a shifter to work, she mused. Aidan had said himself that this Dracin fellow was in such a coupling, and that other shifters had been in the woods, watching their mates.

If that were true, then the logical conclusion was that not only were the shifter-witch matings possible, but also that the witches had freedom. If they could dance around a bonfire for the Devil, then clearly they weren't some drudge, imprisoned in their shifter mate's home.

The thought startled her, and brought a tentative sense of relief. The truth was, her thoughts were consumed with Aidan. And not just about how great a lover he'd be, but what a future with a man like him would entail. Her argument of becoming his slave didn't fly in the face of what she'd seen of him. *Yes, he has a domineering side, which is ridiculously hot, but he's also caring and, even more amazing, willing to listen to me.* How many men could boast that trait? She wasn't stupid. She knew he could easily force—actually, make that seduce—an acceptance of his mark if he chose to. Only an honorable man would wait for her to agree or, in his words, make her ask for it.

Therein lay the danger. He made it seem so simple, so right, which made it all the scarier. She could see herself giving in, and soon if she didn't find a way to escape.

As she lay huddled on the couch under a blanket, she fought the urge to crawl into his bed, where he'd eagerly welcome her, probably naked. She tried to think of a way to escape. He'd left her enough freedom to walk straight out of the cabin right then if she wanted. She could check the place for a broom to use. It would be easy enough to fly off into the night, free of all temptation.

The only thing that wouldn't solve? How to free herself from the feelings Aidan provoked in her. The ones that said, *take me and make me yours forever.*

AIDAN LAY IN BED, hoping against all odds that Sophia would choose to follow him. She didn't, of course, although he grinned when he heard her knocking things around while she cleaned up their dinner plates. She wanted him; he had no doubt of that. He could have had her there in the kitchen too. Her response to his embraces had made that clear. But he wanted more than a simple seduction. *I want her to choose me. Come to me of her own free will and not drugged on my kisses.*

He hoped he'd given her food for thought; he knew she certainly had for him. He hadn't known about some of the things she'd told him. The high infertility and mortality rates, and the idea that she could lose her magic. The simple solution was to not have children. Which, he now understood, would be why his pack discouraged non-shifter pairings. They were too focused on ensuring future generations of their kind.

He wondered how he'd feel if he were in Sophia's shoes. He hadn't known that she'd been adopted, or how important having a family was to her. How would he feel if he were told to either give up those dreams or give up his wolf? The concept frightened him, and it made him better appreciate her feelings. To have magic, something that was a daily part of her life, suddenly gone would make her human. Only for a short time, if his suspicions were correct, but how daunting it would seem. Would he have the courage to say yes if the roles were reversed? He wanted to think that he would—he believed her to be worth the price. Now, if only she would come around to thinking the same of him.

In the meantime, though, she'd left him with a turgid problem that needed to be brought under control. His arousal put him in a precarious position; it weakened his control.

So, he did the only thing he could since he couldn't have her—yet. He wrapped his hand around the throbbing length of his shaft and stroked the velvet-wrapped steel up and down. He wondered as he played with himself if she would touch herself for relief. The thought made semen pearl at the tip of his cock, and he spread the moisture over the head of his shaft, even as he imagined her tongue poking out to lap at it.

Oh, to see Sophia on her knees, her hands wrapped around his prick, her full mouth opening wide to take his rigid length deep. He longed to sink his hands into her luxuriant hair, to feel the warm pressure of her mouth as she sucked him, devouring him like the most delectable of meals.

Aidan groaned and worked his cock faster, his hand fisted tightly around it and pumping frantically. Would she swallow his thick cream, or would she look up at him expectantly and then push her breasts together to receive a personal pearl necklace?

Biting back a cry, he came, but even before his shaft stopped pulsing, it grew hard again.

Unfortunately, only the real thing would satisfy

him now. As Aidan rolled over, trying to find elusive sleep, he wondered what his next step should be. If only he could talk to someone who'd faced the same problem.

Someone like Dracin.

11

Sleep had captured Sophia before she'd found the nerve to search for a broom. When she awoke to the smell of cooking sausage and toast, she couldn't decide if she was happy to be there still, or regretful that she hadn't made her hasty exit in the dead of night.

Sophia stretched and yawned to work the kinks out of her body. She couldn't entirely blame the couch for her poor night's sleep. The main reason stood shirtless and yummy looking in the kitchen. *There should be a law against looking tastier than coffee in the morning,* she thought grumpily as she dragged her ass to the bathroom. No amount of hair and teeth brushing would take care of the dark circles under her eyes, though.

When she came back out again, he smiled at her, fully revealing his pearly whites and deep dimples. She noted that his chiseled jaw was covered in stubble, and she yearned to run her hands through his bed-tousled hair. Immediately her nipples tightened into hard points and moisture creamed her panties. As she took a seat at the table, she tried to avoid looking at him. She was still annoyed at him for walking away from her last night but even more annoyed at herself. She knew her control was crumbling fast. The list of reasons why she should continue to say no to what he offered paled in comparison to the delights her body—and heart—seemed to think she'd gain.

I need to get out of here. Unbelievably enough, he gave her the opening she needed.

"I've got to go into town this morning to grab a few things. I'd bring you with me but"—his eyes twinkled at her—"I don't want you finding a broom and taking off on me."

His statement suggested that if the cabin had been equipped with a broom before, he'd gotten rid of them now. "You're trusting me to stay alone?"

"You agreed to come here with me."

"People change their minds." She shrugged.

He shrugged back, though she could tell the idea of her leaving irritated. Where he'd been jovial when she first woke, his demeanor now darkened as he delivered a plate of breakfast to the table. "Where would you go? I don't get the impression you're an experienced woodswoman, and only an idiot would go hiking off into the wilderness."

Sophia didn't say a word as she took a seat by the plate. Actually, she couldn't because the hard kiss he gave her left her head spinning. Pleasantly so, but the kiss acted as a reminder of why she needed to leave.

Aidan threw on a shirt and left the cabin, taking off in his monster truck. She was surprised that he wasn't going to eat with her. Knowing she had time, she finished every delicious morsel and even cleaned up the dishes before she went on the move. A quick search of the closet revealed a dustpan, the dreaded feather duster but no broom, not even a mop.

Shoot. She could just imagine him snapping them in half, ensuring she was stuck there with him. Sophia glared at the forest around the cabin. Here she was, surrounded by wood. However, the spell to imbue a broom with flight required a straight length with a bristly end. Crooked limbs made for erratic flights and she needed the bristles, which acted as fuel, storing all the magic. Not to mention, the wider head at the back acted like a rudder on a boat

Oh well. Now that her ankle was healed and she had a full belly and a good night's sleep, she felt more than capable of walking. She ignored his statement that civilization resided miles away. He could be lying—even if he didn't seem the type—but what did it matter? She'd eventually find her way out, right?

Somewhere from the depth of her knowledge, a statistic surfaced. The Pine Barrens in New Jersey covered a million acres. A *million*. It was why the mobs were said to dump bodies there—because they'd never be found. She didn't think they'd gone in the direction of New Jersey, but she couldn't be sure of that. And even if they weren't in the Pine Barrens, the forest outside the cabin could still be huge. Easily hundreds, if not thousands of acres.

It gave her pause, but in the end, she decided she still had to try. It was too hard to leave when Aidan was in the cabin—she'd proven that much last night when she'd failed to leave. And he clearly wasn't going to listen to reason and volunteer to take her home. Trying to leave on foot through the woods was the only way this could happen before she lost her resolve and caved into her feelings toward him. She wouldn't survive another night like the previous one. Heck, she probably wouldn't last until dinner if he took off his shirt again.

So, after pulling out her most comfortable walking shoes from her bottomless bag, she set off on her jaunt through the big, scary woods. Following the road would have probably made more sense, but she remembered the way it weaved, so logic dictated if she went in a straight line through the woods, she'd save time, not to mention avoid Aidan when he came back.

Sophia admittedly wasn't much of a nature girl. Her idea of communing with Mother Earth usually consisted of visiting the fruits and vegetable section of the grocery store. But people went hiking all the time. Some even—*ick!*—enjoyed it. How hard could it be?

An hour or so later, sweating and grime-covered, not to mention scratched from slapping branches and brambles in her hair, she cursed aloud, "Stupid forest. Why couldn't they have built a path through it?"

She said a few more choice items under her breath,

most of them shockingly unladylike, but she shut up quickly when she heard the snapping of a branch, a noise that she extraordinarily enough hadn't caused.

Sophia paused mid-step and listened. The annoying sounds of birds singing, accompanied by the constant rustling of tree branches, came to her ears. She chided herself for her fear. *I'm not a little pig, and the only wolf I need to worry about has gone to town.*

Instead of taking another step, she suddenly stopped, paralyzed with fright, for behind her came a low, rumbling growl.

Oh, shoot and double-shoot. I'm going to get eaten.

Sophia debated whether to run, but then she reminded herself of something. *I'm a witch. Like, hello, a stupid wild animal is no match for my magic.* With more confidence than she felt, Sophia whirled around to face the beast stalking her as its next dinner.

Unlike Little Red Riding Hood, she didn't trust the very large wolf that faced her with gleaming yellow eyes. It stood higher than a regular wolf would, its fur a mottled russet and brown, with large teeth better suited to a carnivorous dinosaur.

She had a feeling the beast she faced was a shifter, but to make sure, she tried to send a spell of paralysis. Even with the quickly chanted words and clapping hands completed correctly, the spell was to no avail. The wolf took a step forward.

Sophia swallowed and took a step back while a drop of fear rolled down her spine to the waistband of her jeans. "Um, Aidan, is that you?" she questioned in a wavering voice. She already knew it wasn't. Aidan's wolf was much nicer looking, with dark hair that glinted blue. But perhaps the mention of Aidan's name would make the other shifter think twice about having her for lunch. Sophia took another step back, one the wolf mimicked. She held out her hands in an attempt to look benign, and she tried pleading with it.

"Listen, I'm here with Aidan. He's a wolf shifter just like you. Maybe you know him. Big, tall guy, drives a monster truck?" She ended her rushed speech on a hopeful, questioning note, but the mangy beast just growled and bared even more teeth.

Sophia would have wet her pants if her bladder hadn't frozen tight in fear like the rest of her. Her voice worked just fine, though. When the wolf finally decided to make its move and leaped with a chilling snarl, she screamed at the top of her lungs.

Then she was too busy fighting for her life. Somehow, a necklace of puncture marks didn't sound healthy.

AIDAN, who furiously tracked the weaving and circling path of his none-too-bright-at-that-moment mate, heard her shriek of terror come from closer than he would have thought. With no care for his clothing, he shifted, the fabric tearing in his urgency. His fur was still sprouting even as he leaped toward the terrifying sound of snarls.

He didn't bother concealing his arrival because speed was much more important than stealth. The scent of her fear came to him at the same moment that he caught sight of the perpetrator. *Randy—pack beta and now a dead wolf walking.*

Roaring in fury, Aidan charged and distracted the russet wolf that turned its head from its attempt to rip out Sophia's throat. Without hesitation, Randy braced to meet his charge. Aidan's momentum barreled him right into the other beast, and they tumbled into the underbrush. In a blood-frenzy—Aidan smelled Sophia's injury—he snapped and tore at the other shifter. Caught in the grips of a mindless rage, he wanted to kill Randy, too furious to care about his foe's status as second-in-command. A line had been crossed when Randy had dared harm Sophia.

No one hurts my mate!

12

SOPHIA GINGERLY SAT UP, STILL ALIVE IF SCRATCHED UP from the mangy wolf's claws. And speaking of wolves, Aidan had arrived in the nick of time, the darkness of his fur and evident rage easy to recognize. She watched in terror as the two large beasts wrestled viciously a few paces from her. It never even occurred to her to make her escape while Aidan and the other wolf were locked in battle. She couldn't leave him. What if he was hurt or if the other wolf prevailed and killed him?

A racking shudder went through her at the thought. *He can't die. I won't let him!* But there was nothing she could do, not in such a violent fight that involved such huge snapping teeth and testosterone raging. She could only sit there, feeling helpless, with her knees pulled up and her face pressing into them so she didn't have to witness the carnage in front of her.

Please be okay, please be okay.

When the woods finally fell silent, she chanced a

glance. Aidan's beast held the other pinned by the throat. The wolf that'd attacked her whimpered in submission, and Aidan released him with a slight shake. The wolf remained cowering on the ground, and Aidan turned to give his back, the ultimate insult. He face Sophia and shifted back into his human form as he walked toward her.

Unlike the first time they'd met in the woods, this time she observed his change and processed how impressive it was. Sure, she'd grown used to her own magic by now, but she couldn't change forms like that. The ability was stunning.

And amazing.

But then she was left alone with Aidan fully naked in front of her. He definitely packed an erotic punch. From his broad chest, crisscrossed in more muscles than should be legal, down to a tapered waist and below that... Well, let's just say he put most men to shame.

Sophia couldn't help the heat that suffused her body, even amidst the turmoil. Perhaps because of it. She'd been afraid for her life and this man had saved her. She'd been afraid for *his* life, and relieved beyond belief when he survived. She wanted him like she'd never wanted a man before and she had a feeling if she didn't take what he offered, she'd never find that feeling with anyone else. He was her one chance at what romance books hinted at: the elusive one and only love of her life.

Screw the consequences. They could figure all that

out later, because she needed him, and she needed him *now*.

Her eyes drifted down his body, and right before her mesmerized eyes, his dormant shaft lifted and grew. Her lips unconsciously parted, and she licked them, as her core warmed and moistened in anticipation.

Aidan growled and dropped to his knees, which hid his most interesting body part. "Show me your injuries."

"It's just scratches," she said, looking into his face, which had creased with concern.

"It shouldn't have happened at all," he snapped.

Sophia dropped her head in chagrin, his rebuke stinging, even if truthful. "I'm sorry. I should have stayed in the cabin," she mumbled.

A callused finger tilted her chin up to meet his gaze. "While I agree you shouldn't have left the safety of the cabin, it is also my fault for not informing the pack and, even worse, leaving you alone at all. Although," he said with a glare over his shoulder, "my pack brother should have known better than to attack without asking questions first. Especially considering you're covered in my scent." Aidan stood up and turned around to face the man he spoke of.

As she looked around his legs, Sophia saw that the russet wolf had disappeared and in its place now hunched a naked man. Not a very interesting one either compared to Aidan.

"She's a witch traipsing all over pack land," said the other man.

"She's my mate," growled Aidan.

"Who doesn't wear a mark. And if Jason has anything to say about it, she won't. He won't like this." The other man seemed to gain confidence and stood, unashamed of his nakedness. *He really should cover it,* thought Sophia, given his diminutive size.

Sophia smothered a giggle. This was not a laughing matter, but the whole thing seemed incongruous. Her in the woods, with two naked guys who'd just fought over her? No one would ever believe it.

"I'll speak with Jason soon. If you know what's good for you, you'll keep this to yourself. Don't make me regret letting you live. This is the only warning you'll get. Come near Sophia again, and I will kill you."

With a snarl, the other man shifted back to his wolf shape and bounded off through the woods. The danger gone, Sophia stood and wrapped her arms around Aidan's bare torso. She pressed a cheek to his back and inhaled his scent, allowing herself to fully process what they'd just experienced.

He didn't turn to face her, just gently removed her arms from him and muttered a terse, "Follow me."

Sophia didn't move. The view of his naked buttocks as he stalked away robbed her of speech as it created vividly erotic scenarios in her mind. Her lust, barely in check since she'd met him, simmered to life, and she was done fighting it. Running away wouldn't make her feelings for him disappear. Asking him to take her home wouldn't, either. Whatever strings the universe used to tie them together—claiming bite or not—were stronger than any will she might have to forget him.

Am I nuts?

There were so many unknowns. So much she didn't understand about his kind or about couplings between witches and shifters. What she did know? That there *were* other witch-shifter couples out there, and that meant that it was possible. It could work out. They weren't doomed for failure.

We have time to learn about all this. But now, I need to stop trying to deny that what I feel for him is unlike anything I've ever experienced before and is very likely to be the only chance I have for a love like none other. How stupid would I be to throw it away?

As if her acceptance of her fate had unlocked a dam, pure arousal flooded her. Her breathing came short. A blazing heat consumed her, and she wanted to tear off her clothes and let the fresh air of the forest cool her down. Or, even better, have Aidan lick…

"Would you stop that?" he said in a strained voice. He turned to face her, and she realized he found himself in the same aroused state. Sophia took a step toward him, then another. Screw it. She threw herself at him and tilted her face up to seek his lips. His arms came around her tightly and lifted her, which helped her find them. She proceeded to devour him hungrily.

He, however, was stupidly trying to protest. "Your scratches need tending."

She sucked his lower lip and muttered, "I'm fine."

"This isn't the place—"

"Oh, shut up and make love to me already," she said impatiently.

But the idiot still hesitated, and untangling her arms from around his neck, he set her back. "I might not be able to control myself—to stop myself from biting you. I don't want to do anything you'll regret. I can wait until you're sure."

"Well, I can't wait any longer." She sighed when she saw he wouldn't budge. Funny thing, now that she'd made up her mind, she felt certain she wanted him to claim her. *Now*. She wanted to belong to him forever, consequences be damned.

"For what?" His tone was testy, and his narrowed eyes proved that he wasn't in a playful mood.

She rolled her eyes. "You're going to make me say it out loud, aren't you?"

He crossed his arms over his chest, which only made him appear larger, and Sophia almost melted into a puddle. The man owned way too many muscles.

"Fine. I want to be with you. Are you happy? When I thought you might die back there protecting me, it made me realize I'd probably never find another man who makes me feel the way you do. I'm tired of fighting my own body and heart. Screw what the coven says. Screw the whole interspecies is frowned-upon bullshit. I want you. So, bite me, love me, do what you have to. But, please, Aidan, make me yours."

AIDAN COULDN'T BELIEVE his ears. Despite his bravado, he'd started to believe that he'd been wrong, that Sophia wouldn't come around to him. Especially when he'd returned to the cabin and found it empty.

Yet there they were. The words he'd doubted he'd ever hear had suddenly spilled from her lips. But still, he hesitated. "Don't say it unless you mean it. Once done, we will be bound together forever."

"Do you intend to lock me up and prevent me from continuing my studies as a witch?"

"What? Of course not," he replied indignantly.

With a seductive smile, she closed the space between them and peered up with eyes gone smoky with desire. "Then, in that case, claim me."

A man—and wolf—had only so much willpower. He wouldn't fight her, especially not since he'd wanted this from the first moment he'd met her. He wished only she'd chosen a more comfortable location, but waiting was no longer an option.

He melded his lips to hers in a searing kiss. She melted in his arms, and he hugged her close to him, her plush frame fitting so perfectly against him. Only one thing marred the occasion—she still wore clothes. Not for long. Impatient and too clumsy to undo the buttons to her blouse and jeans, he simply tore them from her. She gasped but not in fear. Nay, his naughty witch with heavy-lidded eyes cried out in pleasure.

"Take me," she panted.

Aidan wanted to move slowly. He wanted to explore every inch of her luscious body. Lick the cream he could smell. Suckle her nipples into hard little berries.

But the moment his fingers touched the slick folds of her sex and flicked across her swollen nubbin, he lost control. And she reveled in it. He turned her around to face a tree and bent her over partway. Through a growl, he said, "Brace yourself."

Her slender fingers splayed against the bark while her bottom lifted toward him temptingly. His cock jumped and throbbed, eager to plow her channel, but he retained enough control to know his size needed to be coaxed in. By gripping his rigid shaft in one hand, he was able to guide it between her buttocks and rub it against her cleft, which wet his bulbous head with her sweet juices.

She mewled and wiggled her bottom at him. "Please, Aidan."

He pushed himself between her moist lips, the heat of her core making him throw his head back in pleasure while his canines descended in anticipation. Inch by inch, he eased into her, the tight walls of her sex squeezing him. She keened and trembled at his slow penetration. Finally, he found himself fully seated inside of her, blissfully slow, but he had to pause. The exquisite feel of her all around him, along with her scent and cries, threatened to make him lose control. But he needed her to climax, for only in the moment of her orgasm would he mark her. He pumped, slowly at first, building momentum as her body adjusted to his size until the satisfying sound of slapping flesh was punctuated with her moans of pleasure.

He leaned forward along the curve of her back, her buttocks fitting nicely in his groin. He nuzzled her back, careful to not hurt her with his wolf fangs. As he tasted her soft skin, working his way up to her neck, he groped forward with his hands and found her breasts hanging heavily. He cupped them and then rolled her nipples between his fingers.

She cried out, and her channel quivered around him. The trembling waves that rippled through her body made him suck in a breath.

"I'm sorry I can't make this last longer," he gasped. "I want you too bad."

She replied by pushing her bottom back into him, sheathing him deep while clamping down on his cock. Aidan gave up the fight. He'd make it up to her later.

Wrapping one arm around her waist, he set the pace, increasing his speed as he pistoned his shaft in and out of her. With her other hand, he pulled her partially up from her bent-over position. His lips touched the vulnerable skin of her nape, as his instinct to bite her, *mark her,* became overwhelming. Tighter and tighter, her channel squeezed him, brought him to the brink, and when she came, screaming and convulsing in shockwaves around his cock, he bit down and tasted her lifeblood.

Ahh, sweetheart, finally you're mine, forever.

13

SOPHIA, LOST IN THE THROES OF PASSION, DIDN'T FEEL any pain when he marked her. On the contrary, when his teeth penetrated, she rolled right into a second orgasm, even more intense than the first. The pleasure consumed her wholly. So much so that she stopped breathing for a moment and her body shattered blissfully into thousands of pieces. Her orgasm was incredible, and it wouldn't stop. Instead, it increased when finally, with a cry that closely resembled a howl, Aidan spent himself inside her, the hot wetness of his seed filling her over and over as her sex spasmed around his cock, wringing every last drop of pleasure from him.

Even more fascinating, she felt the moment their souls touched and melted partially together. Through this intimate link, she could feel Aidan and how much he cherished her, loved her. It sounded way too intense for people who'd just met, but she understood it now. The shifter mating link and its ability to weave two souls together in a way once unimaginable to her. Destiny had determined they were meant to be together, and how long they'd known each other didn't matter. The depths of his emotions awed her, and she swore to herself she'd be worthy of him.

And even better, her magic didn't leave her. If anything, it felt amplified. She felt more powerful in that moment than she'd ever felt before.

She might have blacked out for a second, the intensity of the moment too much for her. The next thing she knew, she found herself cradled in Aidan's naked lap. He used his lips to brush the top of her head, and his arms hugged her tight.

"Are you okay?" he whispered anxiously against her ear through a curtain of hair.

"Of course not," she replied mischievously. His body stiffened, and she understood an unspoken concern. To reassure him, she quickly added, "I'm fine. My magic's fine. It's just that I'm still horny. You didn't think one time was going to cure it, did you?" Under her cheek, his chest rumbled with laughter, and she smiled, too, before kissing the hollow of his throat.

"Wait until you learn that there's no cure for this. You and I will want each other with this intensity until the end of time."

She sat back, looking at him while her heart raced. He hadn't said the words aloud, but it seemed like she'd heard him clearly in her mind.

"You can." His words were again in her mind only, though his chuckle was out loud.

"How?" she asked.

"A true mating benefit. We're joined spiritually as well as physically now."

"What's that mean?"

"We can read some of each other's thoughts and feel strong emotions."

"Really?" Sophia smiled wickedly, then asked, "Can you read what I'm thinking now?" while imagining him licking his way down her body until he was looking up at her from between her legs.

His chest shook with laughter again. "You are one naughty witch. I think that sounds like a plan, but what do you say we adjourn to a more comfortable location first?"

"Mmm, you know what I'd really like is a shower. With you in it."

The words barely left her mouth before he stood, scooped her into his arms, and began jogging through the woods, carrying her as if she weighed no more than a feather. The unconscious display of his strength stirred her passion, and she twined her arms around his neck before she kissed her way along his jaw.

"Sophia," he pled.

"Yes?" she said, not pausing in her light caresses.

"I'd like to make it indoors before I fuck you again, but, damn it, if you don't stop it, I'm going to take you like a rutting animal again."

"Promise? Because I'd really like that," she replied, giggling when he added a burst of speed.

Quicker than she would have believed possible,

considering how long she'd wandered around lost, they made it back to his cabin.

Once inside, he let her slide down his body while keeping his arms around her and holding her close. Both naked, their skin melded together, her breasts squashing against his chest. He kissed her like a starving man, sucking her lower lip before delving deep into her mouth. Their tongues danced together for a while, but an insistent prodding against her lower belly kept distracting her. Pulling back, she reached down to grab him and then wrapped her hand firmly around his thick shaft. Like silk-covered steel, his cock fascinated her, and she wanted to explore its length. But she needed to bathe it first.

Pulling him as if his dick were a leash, she led him into his bathroom, where he'd rigged a shower stall. She wasn't sure how he got water to the cabin. Maybe he had a well. She didn't really care. All that mattered was that when she turned on the faucet, warm water poured out.

There was something about standing in a shower naked with someone that was strangely intimate. Sure, they'd had sex out in the woods. He'd seen her naked, and she'd seen him naked, but in the confined space of the bathtub with the shower curtain drawn, it became more intimate. Not to mention steamy.

Under the hot spray, their mouths found each other, and a frenzy of kissing ensued. It involved a lot of tongue and stroking of bodies. Even with their recent bout in the woods, his cock still poked at her readily, and she gripped him in a wet palm, sliding her hand back and forth, enjoying the hard, thick feel of him. Even naughtier, she wanted to taste him.

She soaped his body quickly. Through their bond, she could feel his amusement at her eagerness, but even more exciting, she could sense his arousal. When she had him clean to her satisfaction—a gesture he'd reciprocated on her body—she positioned him under the spray, which blocked it from hitting her but kept the air hot and steamy. She dropped to her knees in the tub and put herself eye-to-eye with his shaft. As if to say hello, it jerked and a bead formed on the tip. Grasping him tightly around the base, she licked the salty droplet, a move that earned her a groan. Still lapping at him, she looked up and caught her breath. Aidan gazed down at her with smoky eyes. She could see the hunger on his face and, through their link, how much he loved, cherished, and wanted her. A heady sensation, but she had harder things in need of her attention right now.

Opening her mouth wide, she went to work, sliding her wet orifice down the length of his cock. She moaned around her mouthful when his fingers tangled in her wet hair, pulling at it deliciously, the pain heightening her burgeoning desire. She used one hand to hold his cock steady as she sucked and slurped away, the pleasure indicator easy to follow in how his fingers tightened in her hair and his breath came short or, even better, he let loose a groan.

But she wanted him wild, losing his mind like he'd

made her do since the moment they'd met. Her free hand came up to fondle his heavy sac. She kneaded his balls, squeezing them, but it was when she stroked the soft skin right behind that she finally found what she was looking for. He jerked, and the muscles in his thighs tightened.

"Stop before you make me lose it," he growled.

Her response? Suck harder and stroke the sensitive skin hidden by his sac with a firm finger. His hands tried to pull her away, halfheartedly, and still, she suctioned him. She knew the moment of his release had arrived when his whole body went rigid, and with a moaning sigh, he said "Sophia." The spurting warmth in her mouth made her swallow eagerly, even as the throbbing in her pussy intensified; she knew her turn was next. She could read his intent thanks to their bond.

And she couldn't wait.

THERE WASN'T A MAN—OR shifter—alive who wouldn't agree that getting a BJ was one of the best gifts he could be given. Even better when their mate swallowed. But with his pleasure sated, Aidan needed to step up to the plate. He could clearly smell and sense Sophia's desire. The scent was delicious, and it made him hungry. The shower, however, placed too many limitations on them, and he wanted the free range to give her all the pleasure imaginable.

He turned off the water and wrapped a fluffy towel around her. She moved to step out of the tub, but he had her in his arms before her foot could touch the bathroom floor. They kissed the short distance to the bedroom until he tossed her onto the mattress. She bounced and giggled, and the towel fell away to reveal her perfect body—perfect for him at least. He couldn't imagine anything more beautiful than his mate.

Heavy breasts with large puckered nipples, an indented waist, flaring hips, and a rounded tummy he wanted to bury his face in. At the moment, she held her creamy round thighs tightly closed, but he could imagine the pink treasure hidden between them. It was time to become well acquainted with that delight.

He grabbed her ankles and pulled her legs apart, reveling in her soft cry and heavy-lidded eyes. He crawled up the bed to settle himself between her parted legs and take a long look at her pussy. He stroked her short bush, glad she didn't shave it bald. The natural presence of hair was something he liked. Perhaps it was because of his wolf side, or maybe he just liked his pussy old-style. Whatever the case, he thanked his stars as he ran a finger through her curls to the silken slit of her mound.

She shuddered, and wetness coated his finger. She was so ready for him. He hated to torture her, but he wanted to make up for their quickie in the woods, show her the heights he could take her to as her man, her mate.

He moved up her body, pressing forward 'til the

crown of his cock just barely touched her nether lips. She sighed and wiggled her hips, but he stayed just out of reach, only teasing her with light touches. Before she could protest—he could see her brow creasing in frustration—he latched onto one of her nipples and almost accidentally sheathed her when she bucked hard under him.

Her hands came up and grabbed his shoulders, her nails digging in as he sucked and bit at her sensitive peak. She kept bucking under him like a spirited filly, and his recently sated desire came roaring back. How could it not when she moaned so sweetly and her scent filled the air like the most erotic of perfumes?

He pushed her breasts together, lavishing attention on her turgid points, drawing her nipples out with hard sucks that made her thrash. Only when she mewled his name with a drawn-out *please* did he stop the torment. He slid his lips down the rounded and soft skin of her tummy. As if she sensed his objective—she probably could read it through their link—she drew her legs up and wide, exposing herself to him in a way that made his breath catch.

He'd hoped for a lot of things in his mate. A passion to match his own, however, was better than a dream come true. He rubbed his way down over the curve of her belly and nuzzled her soft curls. She twitched and writhed at his touch, her impatience and desire begging for release. He took his time, first tickling with the tip of his tongue the soft skin of her inner thigh. It was only when he transferred his butterfly caresses to the other side that she begged.

"Aidan, please."

He covered her sex with his mouth, and she bucked so hard she almost knocked him off her body. Chuckling at her passionate response, he wrapped his arms around her thighs and locked her down before opening wide to taste her again.

Anchored and unable to thrash, she keened at his touch, and he lost himself in the pleasure of tasting her. Her channel was thick with her cream, and he stabbed his tongue deep, lapping at her inner core. When he switched tactics and suddenly latched onto her swollen, sensitive clit, she came hard almost instantly. Her scream rang out in the room like the sweetest of music, and he flicked at her nub faster. He loosened one hand from where he held her down to delve between her silken folds. He plunged two fingers into her sex, catching the rippling waves of her orgasm. The clutching wetness of her channel affected him greatly.

In torturing her, he tortured himself, and he couldn't take any more. He slid up her body and caught her lips with his as he finally sheathed his cock in one stroke. She fit around him like a tight, moist glove, and he angled himself to plunge deeper, seeking her G-spot. He knew he'd found it when her fingers scrabbled at his back, pulling him closer and scratching him in her frenzy.

"That's it, sweetheart," he murmured against her mouth. "Come for me again."

He kept up his pounding pace, and in short order, she cried out, her pussy squeezing and milking him into orgasm. One last mighty heave and he went rigid, his hot seed spurting inside her.

He had enough presence of mind not to collapse on her and somehow managed to roll without breaking their intimate connection. She snuggled drowsily on his chest, splayed over him decadently.

His arms tightened around her when he heard, not aloud but through their connection, the words, *I love you, Aidan.*

14

Aidan awoke at the brisk knocking that came the morning after a night of loving, the likes of which he could never have imagined. Sophia continued to sleep soundly as he extracted himself from the bed and drew on some pants and a shirt before he walked barefoot to the cabin door.

Opening it, he wasn't surprised to find Randy, accompanied by Teagan, another pack member.

Randy smirked. "Jason wants to see you."

"Just couldn't wait to go running back to him, could you? I told you I'd speak to him, and I meant it."

"He's the pack leader. I owe my allegiance to him, not you. He needed to know," declared the snitch.

"Whatever." Aidan knew there wasn't any point wasting breath with the sycophant who held the beta position in the pack, a post won through ass-kissing and not any real abilities. Aidan pulled out some running shoes and put them over his bare feet.

Straightening, he saw Randy sniff the air and leer at him. "I see someone's been busy. Was she good in the sack?"

Aidan's face hardened. Around shapeshifters, scent always gave them away, and after the loving he'd shared with Sophia, the scent of sex hung heavy throughout the cabin as well as on his skin. A delightful perfume he hoped to wear daily from here on in, but Randy spoiled it with his very presence.

"Do not speak of her disrespectfully, or you'll be going back to Jason in pieces." Aidan offered a mirthless smile as Randy blanched. "Let's go." Aidan wanted out of there quickly before Sophia woke up. He didn't want her getting involved, and what little he knew of his determined mate suggested that she would insist on going with them.

Not if he could help it.

He wanted her safe in case things devolved into a fight, something his gut told him seemed more and more likely.

It was only when he'd reached his truck that he realized only Randy followed him.

"What's Teagen doing?"

Randy spat on the ground before answering. "Making sure your witch stays put. We wouldn't want her wandering around the woods again. Never know what might happen."

Icy fingers walked down Aidan's spine at the implied threat, and ignoring the smaller beta for a moment, he stalked back to Teagen and loomed over him.

"Let's get one thing clear. Touch one fucking hair on her head and I will hunt you down and skin you *alive*."

If Teagen were in wolf form, he would have rolled over on his back and presented his vulnerable belly. As it was, in man shape, he swallowed hard, fear evident in his eyes. "I—I won't touch her."

Aidan gave him one last hard look then followed Randy to his truck. Things didn't bode well, but Aidan refused to give up without a fight. He'd been content until now to allow others dominion in the pack, but if it came down to a battle for dominance, Aidan knew he stood a good chance of winning. He couldn't allow himself to doubt. His future and Sophia's depended on it.

SOPHIA WOKE AND STRETCHED, a smile curving her lips.

What a night!

When she'd decided to give herself to Aidan wholeheartedly, she'd expected pleasure but not the overwhelming contentedness and connection that imbued every inch of her.

I love him.

The words didn't shock her. How could they? They were the truth. She couldn't wait to tell him. She could already imagine his look—fierce, loving, and protective, then turning into smoky desire. Mmm.

She swung her legs out of bed, slightly surprised he wasn't there to greet her with a morning kiss. *Probably making breakfast.*

However, she didn't find him in the kitchen, bathroom, or living room. Becoming concerned, she sat down on the sofa to think where he could have gone at this early hour. *And without telling me.* After a peek out the window, she frowned. Not only was his truck gone but she also caught a glimpse of movement, as a strange man, barely more than a kid really, wearing only jeans, shifted position where he lounged against a tree.

Fear knotted her stomach. She tentatively reached for the connection she'd formed with Aidan the day before. She got a brief impression of anger, not toward her, then danger and fear for her. *Aidan?* She sent a tremulous inquiry at him and thought he hadn't heard, but to her shock, he replied back, loudly.

"Get out of the cabin. The broom's in the woodshed. Fly to your brethren. Now!" Abruptly she found her connection to him cut off, but not before she received a terrible sensation of pain—pain being inflicted on Aidan!

And he expected her to run? Not freaking likely. *He's mine, and I'll be damned before I let him face danger alone.* Sophia snarled as she stalked to the bedroom and rummaged through her bag for clothing more appropriate to flying and invading a pack of shifters.

Magic might not work against shifters, but anger focused her mind, and she suddenly saw ways she could use her power as a force to be reckoned with. With no time like the present, she cast magic toward the door, flinging it open ahead of her and startling the werewolf guard lounging outside.

He recovered quickly and came toward her, hitching his thumbs through his belt loops and sucking in his scrawny chest. "Get back in the cabin."

"Where is he?" she snapped.

"He's been called to explain himself to the pack alpha. Now, get back inside."

Sophia ignored his request. "What are they doing to him? Where are they?"

"Listen, miss, I don't know what's going on. Alls I know is Aidan was supposed to have a talk with Jason, and I'm supposed to make sure you don't go anywhere 'tils they come to a decision."

"Really?" Sophia smiled at him coldly and started drawing on her power. At a time like this, she found herself glad she'd followed the Devil's magic and not the weaker, potion-reliant Wiccan way. Because what she had planned only the dark arts would do. "I'm going after Aidan, so I'm going to give you one chance to get out of my way like a good little boy or else."

The young man drew himself up and puffed out his chest with importance. "I know your witchy powers can't touch me. So, why don't you go inside like I asked you to? I'm the one in charge here."

Sophia rolled her eyes, not surprised at his response. "Fine, have it your way." She may have been a little pleased at having the opportunity to test her new idea.

Attack indirectly. Sophia sent out tendrils of power. She skimmed it along the ground until it touched what she sought. A moment later a large rock came sailing out of nowhere and struck her guard in the back of the head. With eyes rolling back, he slumped to the ground unconscious. She gaped for a second, shocked it had actually worked.

One down, a whole pack to go. Sophia knew her plan was insane, bordering on suicidal, but she couldn't let Aidan face their wrath alone. Especially not since she knew the rift was because of her.

He'd said their mating bond would connect them forever. Well, that meant that she needed to be at his side, in good times and bad.

Hurrying, she went to the woodshed and opened the door. At first, she didn't spot the broom; he'd tucked it in the corner with a tarp over it. But once she found it, she immediately began chanting and imbuing it with the magic she needed to make it fly.

Spell cast, she sat sidesaddle on the wooden handle and gripped it tightly. Catching movement from the corner of her eye, she saw her guard stirring, stupid werewolf genetics healing him quicker than a human. With a cackling laugh that did her witchy heritage proud, she swooped into the air. Only once aloft did she open her connection to Aidan, using it as a beacon to locate him.

Time to save her wolf.

15

"You will renounce the witch," commanded Jason, a barrel-chested man in his early forties. A surly fellow who'd only gotten worse since his wife ran off. Aidan didn't blame her. Six miscarriages and a husband who fucked around didn't exactly scream happy life.

"Can't renounce her. She's my mate."

Whack.

Jason's fist hit him and a murmur went through the crowd of onlookers who'd gathered in the pack club. Aidan bore the brunt of the blow, refusing to show any sign of weakness. It meant a few teeth rattled and coppery fluid coated his tongue. He would have fought back if his arms weren't pinned behind his back, held there by two of his pack brothers. Jason knew he'd never win in a fair fight.

Aidan spat out the mouthful of blood. "Is that the best you can do?" Never mind his face throbbed. Pride kept him cocky. "Have you grown so weak you need someone to hold your opponents down so you can beat on them? Do you also like to kick grandmothers to the ground? Beat up small children? I thought a pack leader was supposed to be the strongest."

"Shut up," snarled Jason, his features turning ruddy as Aidan insulted him.

The fucker deserved it. After all, what had Aidan done to earn such ire? Simply spoken the truth that he'd mated a witch. For some reason, Jason had taken it personally and demanded Aidan sever the bond. When Aidan refused to obey, the beating started.

"Truth hurt?" Aidan refused to cow down before this fucker.

"The truth is you mated a witch. You took her without permission, disregarding the fact that only purebloods are accepted as mates, fated or not."

"Then accept my offer to leave. You don't even have to exile me. I can live without the pack, but we both know I won't thrive without my mate."

Jason's gaze narrowed. "I can't allow that either. Wolf and witches aren't ever to join."

"Says who?"

"Says one of the secret laws handed down to me when I became alpha."

Secret laws? Aidan never heard of them and truly didn't give a fuck. A cold smile stretched his lips. "Then perhaps it's time we changed those laws. Perhaps it's time this pack had a new leader too." The moment he said it, he knew his fate was sealed. To save face, Jason would have to fight.

Quickly, he sent Sophia a message, telling her to run. He shoved all of his worry and urgency into the request. He needed her to listen because he had to believe she would find safety. It was the only way he could focus on the coming fight and concentrate on trying to stay alive.

Before she could reply and argue, he cut his link to her, then returned to poking the agitated mutt in front of him.

"Let's go, tough guy. You and me. One on one."

"You don't get to challenge me. You're standing here accused." Jason blustered.

Aidan couldn't help but smirk. "Accused of what? Calling you out on your bullshit? What's wrong, Jason? Afraid everyone will see what a pussy you are if we fight? A real alpha can enforce his laws himself."

"Enough! I'm done listening to you. Take him away and prepare him for execution." Jason blew spittle in his agitation. His eyes glowed, a fanatic wildness lighting them and deepening Aidan's dread.

"Now hold on there a second," interjected an older member of the pack. "This ain't right. And not just the fact you got two guys holding the boy so you can smack him. If Aidan has found his true mate, who cares what her blood is? Tradition says once a mate is found, it's 'til death do you part. It's not the boy's fault he didn't find himself a nice bitch. If you don't want a witch in the pack, then banish him, I say, but you can't kill him over something he can't control."

"Especially not with his hands bound," yelled another in the crowd.

"Let him go so he can defend himself. It's the pack way. Or have you forgotten, *alpha*?" the third fellow accused with a hint of a sneer at the end.

A rumbling assent came from the gathered shifters, and the grip on Aidan's arms loosened with indecision.

"You want me to prove my merit, then fine," Jason snapped. "I'll kick his ass myself. Let him go."

Figures. He holds me down to beat the crap out of me, and when he thinks I'm weakened enough, he decides to wolf up. Should have beaten me longer, thought Aidan, a feral smile lighting his face.

The grips holding him back disappeared and Aidan found himself free. He flexed his arms to circulate blood through them.

Jason approached him, muscles bulging under the fat that a slovenly lifestyle had graced him with.

Time to make him work for his job. Aidan crouched slightly and held himself ready as he and Jason paced a cleared area, the other wolves forming a circle of spectators.

"I'm here to help, Aidan!"

He lost his focus when Sophia's voice called out in his head. Jason's first blow connected, and Aidan's face snapped to the side. The punch dazed him, but not enough to miss his mate's grand entrance.

The doors to the club blew open with a resounding crash, and in the sunlit doorway stood his witch, a light breeze lifting the tendrils of her hair as she stood with one hand on her cocked hip while the other held his ratty broom like a staff.

He cursed, even as he held back a rueful smile. *That's my witch.* New strength and adrenaline rushed through him. With Sophia on the scene, she was officially in danger, so now nobody in the room stood a chance.

A wolf will protect his mate at all costs.

Sophia hid her trepidation with a show of power and intimidation, but she couldn't help the cry that escaped her when she saw the blood on Aidan's face. "Aidan!"

He glowered at her, speaking in her head alone so others wouldn't overhear. *"I told you to escape."*

"I couldn't leave you." Her words made him smile and shake his head.

"Oh, sweetheart."

"Get her," screamed Jason.

"Touch her and die!" Aidan growled.

Most in the room didn't move, but that still left three shifters coming at her, one swapping his human shape for a wolf one. Using the logic she'd acquired from the cabin, she drew on the power and used it to lift... *Nothing. Shoot.* The room held only bodies, no furniture.

So, when the first wolf reached her, she used the only weapon in her possession, her broom, and whacked it over the nose, which stunned it into sitting. With a terrifying roar, Aidan tackled the other two men who thought to lay a hand on her. The meaty sound of his fist hitting their faces told her he had them occupied so she could concentrate on her current problem.

The wolf in front of her recovered from its surprise and advanced on her. It snarled and showed a muzzle full of large and sharp teeth. Sophia chanted and drew in more magic. Her broom thickened in her grasp, turning into a baseball bat, a much easier weapon to swing.

The wolf didn't stop. He obviously didn't know about her trophies back home for most hits on her softball team three years running. She only cringed after she connected with the wolf's head. Rock-throwing was one thing. Swinging a bat and feeling the shock of connecting from her hands right up to her shoulders was another. But she succeeded. With a whimper, the wolf skulked away on unsteady feet.

Sophia waved the bat menacingly at the still-watching crowd. "Any other takers?" She managed to swallow her sigh of relief when no one stepped forward to her challenge. A short-lived relief, it turned out, when arms wrapped around her from behind to trap her. *Shoot.* Getting caught hadn't figured into her plans.

"Drop the bat, or you'll find out how it feels to die with crushed ribs," growled the voice from behind her.

Sophia dropped the bat with a thunk. *So much for rescuing Aidan. I think I might have made things worse.*

"I've got your witch slut, Aidan," her captor announced triumphantly.

Aidan untangled himself from the two bodies he'd used as punch test dummies. "Let her go, Jason. Your fight is with me."

"Oh, I intend to fight you, right after I take care of your bitch." Jason removed one of his arms from around her and placed his hand against her throat. A sharp pain pricked at her skin.

Oh, this really isn't good.

Things might have gotten really ugly at that point if it hadn't been for the arrival of two new players.

"You would execute a coven member?" A female voice asked in a how-dare-you tone. "One of our own, for no other crime than being caught up in a shifter mating bond—one caused by your kind? I think not. Dracin, darling, if you please."

The woman didn't pause to allow anyone in the room to reply. Sophia felt the cold tingle of alien magic creeping into the room, and Jason's vise-like arm and clawed hand released her. A second later—actually more like a millisecond—Aidan's arms embraced her, and she clung to him, grateful to find them both alive.

Curiosity made her turn to see who had rescued them. At first, her attention was caught by a floating Jason, his eyes wide in fright, his mouth working but without any sound. *How strange. I thought magic couldn't affect shifters?*

Behind the bad alpha's dangling legs, Sophia saw a stud—seriously, he almost put Aidan to shame with his well-over-six-foot lanky frame and wavy blonde hair. His bearing screamed Viking warrior, which made the soft, sappy look he bestowed on a petite woman beside him all the more incongruous. Sophia mentally made the connection based on what Aidan had told her of the shifter who had befriended him. Thus, if the man was Dracin, then the woman by default was Clarabelle, a witch like her. A very pregnant one, too, judging by her bulging belly.

"What is he?" she asked Aidan when she realized who wielded the magic holding Jason.

"Dragon."

Her eyes widened. There hadn't been any lessons on dragons in her studies, because they weren't thought to exist. *"They're real?"*

"You're looking at one right now. He's the one making Jason look foolish."

Dragons existed, and they wielded magic. It explained the alien feel of it, and, even more astonishing, the fact that it affected shifters. Fascinating.

"What would you like me to do with this mongrel, Belle?" asked Dracin, his tone bored.

"I don't think he has the brain capacity to accept what can't be changed."

"I will kill him, then."

Aidan spoke up. "If you kill him, much as he deserves it, my pack might take issue, the whole honor thing. Is there not a way we can neutralize him instead and send him on his way?"

With a curt nod, Dracin raised his hands, and once again, Sophia felt the cool alien magic tickle along her skin. In the blink of an eye, Jason disappeared, and in his place stood a coyote with mangy fur.

Clarabelle shooed the ugly beast. "Bad guy, be gone, and do not return to bother my new friends, or I'll make you into a fur stole."

Sophia bit back a giggle at her words as the coyote, formerly known as Jason, took off scurrying and yipping.

"Now does anybody else want to dispute Aidan and Sophia's bond?" Clarabelle placed her hands on her hips and gave the rest of the pack a stern look, kind of marred by her round belly and glowing cheeks. However, the impressive Dracin, glowering behind her, appeared quite effective, for there was a lot of shaking heads.

"Well then, now that we've settled this, I'm hungry. Sophia, you come with me while Aidan and his pack choose a new alpha. We have much to discuss."

Sophia turned to Aidan with questioning eyes. "Will you be okay? They won't try to hurt you, will they?"

Aidan's eyes crinkled at the corners, and he gave her a grin. "I think we'll be all right from here on. If not, you can come back and beat them with your club." He hugged her tightly and lifted her for a deep kiss, which left her flushed and panting. "I'll come get you when I'm done here." Another hard kiss sent her libido spinning wildly, and she wanted to ask why they couldn't just skip everything and go find a soft bed for sinning—heck, even a wall somewhere would do. But a tug on her arm from Clarabelle and shifters converging on Aidan talking in low voices made her put those plans on hold.

Besides, she did have to admit to some curiosity about Clarabelle and her shifter husband. Upon seeing Clarabelle, Sophia realized she'd seen her around and usually in the company of her superiors. Apparently, Clarabelle had retained some sort of status in the coven, even though she'd gone against custom and married outside their ranks.

It seems I still have much to learn about the world. Starting with the real reason shifter and witch pairings were frowned upon. Hopefully, Clarabelle would answer her many questions.

Far away from the pack and their violent methods, Dracin led the way, his fierce scowl, along with his formidable size, making people on the sidewalk of the small town give them a wide berth. Bemused, Sophia followed them to a greasy spoon down the street.

Their conversation, over an obscene amount of food, most of which Clarabelle ate under Dracin's doting eye, proved more than interesting and answered a lot of questions even as it raised more. Secrets, so many secrets.

Sophia's eyes grew wider and wider. At one particular revelation, she even giggled. *Oh, I wonder what Aidan will think of that.*

The talk with the other witch did assuage a lot of Sophia's trepidations about her future. Aidan was right, the loss of magic was only for the duration of a shifter pregnancy. And Sophia's teacher had been wrong. It turns out, the reason that a witch loses her powers is because the magic is protecting the child and the mother. Witches are actually very successful at having shifter babies.

Sophia couldn't believe it.

Clarabelle and Dracin had a good laugh when Sophia revealed she'd believed the mating bite would turn her into a mindless sex slave. "If anything, it makes *him* one," Clarabelle teased, jerking a thumb toward her adoring dragon.

"So the pairings aren't banned, just discouraged?" Sophia asked for a third time, trying to wrap her head around everything Clarabelle had told her.

"While the coven might not like witches mating with shifters, they can't exactly prevent the bond from happening. When it's meant to be, nothing can stop it," Clarabelle explained. "Count yourself lucky, though, there was a time when you would have been tossed from the coven. It almost happened to me."

"They would have been stupid to dump you. You're one of their best witches," murmured her husband.

"Bah, we both know it's because they love having the prestige of claiming a magic-wielding dragon as their ally." She leaned against him with a smile.

He snorted. They truly were adorable, but even better, seeing them together gave Sophia hope, despite all that had happened.

As they exited the diner, Sophia couldn't help but smile seeing Aidan striding up the street. Happiness brimmed within her at the sight of him. He truly meant the world to her.

She ran to him, her heart bursting with love. He returned her happy grin and opened his arms wide. He was big, bad-boy putty for a little, round witch. Sappy but true, and she wouldn't change it.

"So, what happened?" she asked after he finished planting a whopper of a kiss on her lips, one that her tremble.

"We chose a new alpha."

"That was quick," stated Dracin, who'd arrived with Clarabelle.

"Jason had been pissing the pack off for a while. Problem was the other alpha potentials in the pack didn't want to step in."

"Got roped in, did you?" Dracin laughed.

Sophia gaped up at Aidan. He was an alpha?

"Nope. I made my brother, who arrived late as usual, take the job. Since he's twice my size and meaner, no one argued."

"But why didn't you keep it?"

"I've got a feeling being mated with a witch is going to keep me plenty busy."

"You've got that right," chimed in Clarabelle with a tinkling laugh. "Well, now that everything is settled, it's time for us to leave. Don't worry; we'll visit again soon. I'm sure you have a ton more questions, just remember, no telling anyone what I've told you. Well, anyone except your mate." Clarabelle put a finger to her lips. "I have to say it will be nice to be able to talk to another witch with a shifter of her own. I'd like to do a survey on sizes."

"Belle," growled Dracin, a forbidding look on his face.

"What's wrong with talking about truck sizes?" asked Clarabelle, her innocent look marred by the naughty twinkle in her eye. She turned to Sophia and slipped her a piece of paper. "If you need anything, call me. I live only a short flight away."

"I will," said Sophia. They exchanged goodbyes and watched the other couple walk to a truck that could have been the twin of Aidan's. Another boy with his toy. Funny, she'd have to revise her assumption that only guys with little dicks bought them because she now knew first-hand that little did not apply in his case.

"Let's go home," Aidan said, slinging an arm around her shoulders.

Sophia liked the sound of that. To make the trip back more interesting, she tested his skills of concentration—in other words, how well he could drive while she gave him a hand job.

She kept expecting him to pull over and have his way with her, but with steely-jawed determination, he got them to the cabin.

Only once they got inside did she realize that something was amiss. Of course the fact that he yanked her down on his lap—facedown—and yanked down her pants to give her a firm whack was a pretty good clue.

"Hey!" she yelped. "What's that for?"

"That was for not listening and coming to find me." His hand came down again on her ass with a resounding thwack, which burnt but also, to her surprise, made her pussy clench and dampen. "That one was for scaring the hell out of me barging into a room of shifters like that. Do you have any idea how many years I lost off my life? And this," he said as he slapped her lightly on her burning hot ass and then slid his hand between her fiery cheeks to stroke her, a move she agreed with by moaning, "is for being so goddamn brave and lovable."

As quickly as she'd found herself over his knee, she found herself astride him, his cock sheathed inside her ready channel. He placed his hands around her waist, dictating the rhythm, which buried his prick deep into her while somehow making her clit rub against him, pleasurably so.

Sophia looked him in the eye, those blazing orbs that shone with such emotion that she had to reply. "I love you too."

At her words, he wrapped his arms around her to hug her tightly, and she buried her face in his neck. She was overcome, for through their link she could sense everything he felt: fear, relief, and a love so powerful he'd die for her.

"*I love you, Aidan,*" she projected to him their mental connection. "*And, no matter what, we'll be together, forever.*"

Wrapped tight, they still moved together in an erotic pattern, their bodies melded, his rod still pumping her wet sex. At the brink of orgasm, enough of her witchy side came out that she had to say, "And this is for treating me like a girl." She bit down hard on the soft skin at the base of his neck and then sucked it.

With a bellow, he reared up under her, his cock plowing deep as he shot his cream in hot spurts inside her. It was enough to send Sophia over the edge with screams of her own pleasure.

A pleasure they repeated over and over as they tried to outdo each other with sexual antics, attempting to prove who loved the other the most. It ended in a blissful, exhausted draw.

EPILOGUE
SIX MONTHS LATER...

Sophia knew she was pregnant within hours of making love. It was kind of hard to miss because her magic disappeared as if sucked into a dark hole. Aidan found her in the bathroom sniffling and laughing.

"Sweetheart, what's wrong?" He dropped to his knees beside her, where she sat on the tile floor.

She said it bluntly. "I'm pregnant."

"Are you sure?"

Sophia answered with a dark look.

"Oh, yeah, I guess your magic disappeared. It's all right, though. It'll only be for a few months. I promise to take very good care of you." The jerk looked so smugly happy she wanted to hit him. Although she'd expected this for a while, given how often they made love.

"I know you will," she said as she smiled while leaning over to kiss him. "I didn't mean to cry. I just didn't expect it to be so sudden. Can you believe we're going to be parents?" After her talk with Clarabelle, she'd felt much more hopeful about having a future family with Aidan, but she thought she'd have more time to get used to the idea of losing her magic for a bit.

"I can't wait to be a dad. I'll teach the little pup all kinds of stuff."

Sophia smiled impishly. She couldn't say why she'd waited to tell him this little tidbit, but surprising him with it now proved great fun. "Oh, about the pup thing. Remember that talk I had with Clarabelle at the diner? Well, there's one thing that the books don't mention about shifter and witch babies."

"What?" Aidan's face creased in concern.

"We'll need to do some special baby proofing because there's a strong chance we won't be having a puppy."

"I'd love a little witch like you."

"Nope, think again. Have you wondered about where dragons come from? A shifter who can wield magic, so rare as to be thought non-existent."

"You're saying..." Aidan's wide eyes told her that it was taking him a moment to put two and two together.

"Apparently, a true mate bond between a shifter and a witch means there is a strong chance this baby will be a dragon. How cool is that?"

Apparently, she'd find out his thoughts on the matter later. Her mate blanched and passed out cold. Sophia giggled. Personally, she hoped the child was a dragon so they would have not only their daddy's shifting abilities, but also magic like its mother.

Waking Aidan up in the only pleasurable way she could think of—naked, of course—she smiled. Life was absolutely perfect. She loved Aidan more and more as she grew to know him, and the love he showered her with in return made all her previous trepidations seem so foolish.

And to think, she'd found her true mate and true love because of a broomstick breakdown. It only went to show you that you never know when or where love will strike, but when it was meant to be, nothing—not even a stubborn witch—could stop it.

***The end of Broomstick Breakdown but are you curious about Dracin and Clarabelle? Check out their story in Dragon's Belle.

www.ingramcontent.com/pod-product-compliance
Lightning Source LLC
LaVergne TN
LVHW031540060526
838200LV00056B/4588